Acclaim for Hard Case  of ... !

"*Money Shot* is a stunner, careening along with a wild, propulsive energy and a deliciously incendiary spirit. Laced with bravado and loaded up with knockabout charm, Christa Faust's Hard Case debut is the literary equivalent of a gasoline cocktail."
—*Megan Abbott*

"I was sucked into the tight, juicy *Money Shot*, from the ripping car trunk start to the hard-pumping climax. This novel is so convincing that you want to believe Faust has been an oversexed, naked killing machine, at least once."
—*Vicki Hendricks*

"*Money Shot* is smart, stylish, insightful, fast-paced pulp fiction with razor sharp humor and a kick-ass heroine. Christa Faust is a super crime writer."
—*Jason Starr*

"*Money Shot* makes most crime novels seem about as exciting as the missionary position on a Tuesday night. The results are stunning."
—*Duane Swierczynski*

"Wonderfully lurid, with attitude to spare and a genuine affection for the best of hardboiled traditions. Christa Faust is THE business."
—*Maxim Jakubowski*

"Christa Faust writes like she means it. *Money Shot* is dark, tough, stylish, full of invention and builds to one hell of a climax."
 — *Allan Guthrie*

"Christa Faust proves she can run with the big boys with this gritty thriller set in the darkest places of the porn industry. I loved it!"
 — *McKenna Jordan, Murder By the Book*

"Never has an avenging Angel been sexier. *Money Shot* leaves you spent and wanting more."
 — *Louis Boxer, founder of NoirCon*

We had been driving through dusty Mexican nothing for so long, I would have gotten white-line fever if there had been any lines on the rutted dirt road. When we passed a dead car, it seemed way more exciting than it should have. A sad cluster of cement-block houses seemed like a bustling town. After the sun went down, I started to see pairs of bright, reflective eyes watching from the scrub brush on the sides of the road.

Then finally lights in the distance. Strobes in gaudy headache colors and way too much neon, like an impossible fever dream after the sensory deprivation of the dark desert. Our destination turned out to be this weird lost fragment of Vegas imprisoned behind barbed wire. A maximum security Señor Frog's.

A razorwire fence ran all the way around the place with a sliding gate standing open. The front of the long, narrow building was all molded to look like rock, with fake plastic orchids sticking out at random intervals and several small waterfalls spilling into scummy plastic basins full of greenish American pennies. A big throbbing red sign read CLUB OASIS and flickering neon women shifted their glowing hips robotically from side to side.

"Is this a strip club?" I asked, frowning at the bored-looking guy with body armor and an AK47 who waved us into the fenced parking area.

"It's an anything-you-can-afford club," Hank replied...

**SOME OTHER HARD CASE CRIME BOOKS
YOU WILL ENJOY:**

MONEY SHOT *by Christa Faust*
ZERO COOL *by John Lange*
SHOOTING STAR/SPIDERWEB *by Robert Bloch*
THE MURDERER VINE *by Shepard Rifkin*
SOMEBODY OWES ME MONEY
by Donald E. Westlake
NO HOUSE LIMIT *by Steve Fisher*
BABY MOLL *by John Farris*
THE MAX *by Ken Bruen and Jason Starr*
GUN WORK *by David J. Schow*
FIFTY-TO-ONE *by Charles Ardai*
KILLING CASTRO *by Lawrence Block*
THE DEAD MAN'S BROTHER *by Roger Zelazny*
THE CUTIE *by Donald E. Westlake*
HOUSE DICK *by E. Howard Hunt*
CASINO MOON *by Peter Blauner*
FAKE I.D. *by Jason Starr*
PASSPORT TO PERIL *by Robert B. Parker*
STOP THIS MAN! *by Peter Rabe*
LOSERS LIVE LONGER *by Russell Atwood*
HONEY IN HIS MOUTH *by Lester Dent*
THE CORPSE WORE PASTIES *by Jonny Porkpie*
THE VALLEY OF FEAR *by A.C. Doyle*
MEMORY *by Donald E. Westlake*
NOBODY'S ANGEL *by Jack Clark*
MURDER IS MY BUSINESS *by Brett Halliday*
GETTING OFF *by Lawrence Block*
QUARRY'S EX *by Max Allan Collins*
THE CONSUMMATA
by Mickey Spillane and Max Allan Collins

CHOKE HOLD

by Christa Faust

A HARD CASE CRIME BOOK
(HCC-104)
First Hard Case Crime edition: October 2011

Published by

Titan Books
A division of Titan Publishing Group Ltd
144 Southwark Street
London SE1 0UP

in collaboration with Winterfall LLC

If you purchased this book without a cover, you should know that it is stolen property. It was reported as "unsold and destroyed" to the publisher, and neither the author nor the publisher has received any payment for this "stripped book."

Copyright © 2011 by Christa Faust

Cover painting copyright © 2011 by Glen Orbik
Author photo by Jim Ferreira

All rights reserved. No part of this book may be reproduced or transmitted in any form or by any electronic or mechanical means, including photocopying, recording or by any information storage and retrieval system, without the written permission of the publisher, except where permitted by law.

This book is a work of fiction. Names, characters, places, and incidents either are the products of the author's imagination or are used fictitiously, and any resemblance to actual events or persons, living or dead, is entirely coincidental.

Print edition ISBN 978-0-85768-285-7
E-book ISBN 978-0-85768-405-9

Cover design by Cooley Design Lab
Design direction by Max Phillips
www.maxphillips.net

Typeset by Swordsmith Productions

The name "Hard Case Crime" and the Hard Case Crime logo are trademarks of Winterfall LLC. Hard Case Crime books are selected and edited by Charles Ardai.

Printed in the United States of America

Visit us on the web at www.HardCaseCrime.com

For Chris Nowinski. Keep fighting.

ACKNOWLEDGEMENTS

I couldn't have written this book without a good corner. Special thanks to Charles DeVos, Keenan Lewis, Paul Booe, Matt F'n Wallace, David Ferguson, Eddie Muller, Jimmie Romero, Mark Hardiman, Martyn Waites, Gokor Chivichyan, Gene LeBell, Allan "Pimp Daddy" Guthrie and Charles Ardai, the world's best literary cutman.

CHOKE HOLD

1.

Do the things you've done in the past add up to the person you are now? Or are you endlessly reinvented by the choices you make for the future? I used to think I knew the answer to those questions. Now, I'm not so sure.

I was cutting a slice of lemon meringue pie and watching the door out of the corner of my eye when my past walked into the forgotten desert diner where I'd been waiting tables.

"Angel?"

No one had called me by that name in ages, but when I heard that familiar, sand-blasted South Side voice, I'll admit I felt a tiny fishhook tug in my heart. I used to love hearing that voice say my name. Then I hated it. Right now, I didn't know how to feel about it.

The last time I saw Thick Vic Ventura, it wasn't pretty. Neither was he. Twenty years of crank had cooked him down to bones and ashes. That was nearly two years ago, in another lifetime. I don't know what the hell I was expecting to see when I turned to face that voice, but what I did see grabbed hold of the hook with both hands and twisted.

I saw the ghost of the old Thick Vic. What little was left of his hair had gone steely gray, chopped short by an unskilled hand. His face looked ten hard years older than it should have but the young Vic was still there in his eyes. The same Vic I'd fallen for, back when we both believed that nothing really bad could ever happen to either one of us. Standing there by the register with his hands in his pockets, he looked clean and earnest. He'd put fifteen healthy pounds on his lanky frame and his skin looked warm and pink, like it actually had red, living blood running underneath. His dark eyes looked calm and sane and more than a little melancholy. I wondered what he saw when he looked at me. I had no fucking idea what to say to him.

"Hey, Vic," I eventually said, for lack of anything better.

For a long, uncomfortable moment, neither of us spoke. I looked down at the cheap yellow filling leaking from the slice of pie on the plate in my hand. Vic looked everywhere but at me. He was the one who spoke first.

"I heard…well…" He paused, pulled his hands out of his pockets, looked down at them and then put them back in. "I heard a lot of crazy rumors about…what happened."

That line of conversation went nowhere fast. What was I supposed to say? *Well, Vic, I was raped, shot and left for dead so I hunted down the bastards who did it and killed them in cold blood.* That sort of thing doesn't exactly make for nice casual catch-up chat.

"You look good," I said. At first I just said it because I needed to say something, but once it was out, I realized that I meant it.

He shrugged and cocked his head with a self-deprecating smirk that was vintage Thick Vic.

"Yeah well," he said. "I'm not trying to kill myself with a needle anymore. I've been sober for a year and two months. This time I think it's really gonna take."

I thought maybe I should say something like *congratu-*

lations, but wasn't sure, so I said, "How did you find me?" instead.

"I didn't." Vic looked over at the corner booth and then down at his hands. "See that kid sitting over there."

I looked over at the kid Vic was talking about. He was barely eighteen. Broken nose but still way too handsome for his own good. Intense hazel eyes and dark hair buzzed down to the scarred scalp. Lean, athletic build under an expensive white t-shirt printed with trendy rococo designs, silver skulls and wings. His long, sinewy arms were already sleeved in unimaginative tattoos. There was a red and black motorcycle jacket slung over the back of the booth and a brain-bucket style helmet on the table beside him. He was trying a little too hard and wore bad-ass like a brand new pair of boots that hadn't quite broken in yet. He'd ordered nothing but black coffee and flirted with me every time I came around to fill his cup. Told me he was waiting for someone, but not a girl because I was all the woman he'd ever need. Cocky, like some hot young gun who thinks he doesn't need Viagra for his first scene. But underneath the bad-ass and the heavy-handed Lothario charm, I got the feeling that he was anxious about something.

"What about him?" I asked.

Vic wiped his dry lips with the pad of his thumb and swallowed hard.

"That's my kid," he said.

"Your *kid*?" I frowned.

Vic nodded, smile fading.

"I've never met him." He wiped his thumb across his lips again. "I mean, at the time I knew that Skye was knocked up, but she told me she was gonna get rid of it."

"Skye?" I asked. "You mean Skye Blue?"

Vic shook his head. "Skye West."

"Natural blonde, kind of a hippychick amateur look? Shot mostly for Metropolis but wouldn't do girl/girl?"

"Yeah, that's her."

"No shit," I said, looking back at the kid in the corner booth.

Now that Vic had mentioned it, the kid did bear more than a passing resemblance. He was a few inches shorter, a little prettier and much more muscular than his beanpole father but the crooked, charming smile and that cocky, big dick swagger should have been a dead giveaway.

"I found out about him five years ago," Vic said. "But at the time I was too strung out to care. My life is different, now, so…" Again, that familiar self-deprecating smirk. "I got no idea what to say to him."

I didn't either, so I said nothing.

"Well…" Vic said.

"You really had no idea I was here?" I asked. "Your kid just happened to pick this diner to meet you?"

"Small fucking world, eh? Of all the gin joints in all the towns…" More silence, then, "I'd like to see you again, Angel."

And there it was. I had kinda seen it coming but it still caught me off guard. We weren't exactly in love back in the day, but I suppose it was as close to love as a couple of callow, narcissistic twenty-somethings who fuck other people for a living can ever really be. Anyway it's the closest I've ever been. Whatever you call the way I used to feel about

Thick Vic, I was sure I'd buried all those feelings the day I kicked him to the curb. Right around the time that kid in the corner booth had been conceived.

"Look," Vic continued. "I know you got no reason to give me the time of day, not after the way I fucked everything up between us. But I just want a few minutes of your time, to make amends."

"Amends?" I looked over at the old guy at the counter, waiting for his pie. He was starting to look annoyed. "It's ancient history, Vic."

"Indulge me, Angel," Vic said. "It's part of my recovery."

The old charm was pretty threadbare but it still made me smile despite myself.

"Is a blow job for old time's sake part of your recovery too?" I asked.

He cracked a grin that took years off his weathered face.

"Come on." He put his hand to his heart, mock offended. "What kind of guy do you think I am?"

"I know exactly what kind of guy you are," I told him. "That's the problem."

"Just a few minutes, Angel," Vic said. "Please? The blow job is optional."

I laughed and rolled my eyes.

"Go talk to your kid," I told him. "I'm off at midnight, okay?"

He looked back at the kid and his smile evaporated. The kid was drumming on the table and looking out the window.

"Miss?" said the man waiting for pie, one gnarled finger in the air.

"Go on, willya?" I said to Vic. "You'll be fine."

I walked down to the end of the counter and set the pie in front of the old man, who scowled down at it as if it were the pie's own fault that it had taken so long to arrive. I turned to grab the coffee, surreptitiously watching Vic as he made his way over to the corner booth. He stood there with his back to me, shoulders hunched and uncomfortable under his beat-up leather jacket. He was saying something I couldn't hear. The kid stood and offered his hand.

As I poured coffee for the old guy, Vic looked down at the kid's offered hand and then slowly reached out to take it. They exchanged an awkward handshake and then Vic let go and reached up to push back long hair fifteen years gone in a nervous gesture that was painfully familiar. The kid was looking up at Vic like he was Santa Claus and not really paying attention to the three jittery Mexican guys who walked right past the "Please Wait To Be Seated" sign. I was staring into the mouth of the coffee carafe and wondering if I might actually fuck Vic again after all when one of those Mexican guys made the choice for me. He pulled out a gun and shot Thick Vic in the back.

2.

For a moment after Vic was shot, nothing happened. Vic pulled an instant, boneless pratfall so goofy-looking that I almost believed he was just horsing around. The rest of us stood frozen in place like children caught up in a game of red-light/green-light. My ears were buzzing and my heartbeat seemed like the loudest sound in the room. The kid was wearing a substantial portion of the contents of Thick Vic's abdomen, staring bug-eyed at the mess all over his expensive t-shirt. The Mexican guys were looking back and forth at each other. The shortest one all flushed and pissed off. The shooter with an indifferent *whatever* kind of expression like a teenage son about to be lectured for staying out too late. The tallest but obviously youngest of the trio looking queasy and ready to bolt. Finally, the shortest guy spoke up. When he spoke, I realized how young they really were. My high school Spanish was useless in deciphering the angry barrage of slang and profanity.

The short, swearing kid was bleached blond and manic with a tough, wiry build that he flung around in hyper-exaggerated rap video gangster body language. He was clearly jacked up on something much stronger than diner coffee. The bored-looking shooter was darker skinned and a little Asian around the eyes, an adolescent rash of pimples across his high cheekbones. He seemed the least trashed and the most dangerous. He shrugged and pointed his gun at Vic's kid.

The third Mexican started to say something. He was tall and awkward and looked like he still had several years to go before his first legal American lap dance. He was wired and terrified, eyes jumping and jittering like shiny beetles in their sockets.

"Shut the fuck up, man," the short guy snapped in unexpectedly perfect English, adding a second gun to the mix but not sure where to point it.

Vic's kid, who up until that moment had been standing there clenching his fists and slowly flushing deeper and deeper red until his face matched his gory shirt, let out a wordless howl and launched himself at the bored-looking shooter.

The shooter put a wild stray bullet into the dessert case as the two of them went down hard. Vic's kid had the shooter's gun hand locked up and stretched away from his body while the shooter twisted and flailed, using his free hand to punch the kid repeatedly in the back of the head. There was a sudden crisp snap and the shooter screamed, his gun skittering away and sliding under a nearby booth.

The tall, awkward kid had his own gun out by then, but he held it like a venomous reptile, one that might bite him if he wasn't careful. The short, pissed-off guy was shouting and trying desperately to regain control over the rapidly deteriorating situation. He was clearly the brains of the operation, which didn't bode well for whatever plans these three had made. Especially the part of the plan that involved bringing trouble into Duncan's Diner.

Duncan chose that moment to pop up in the pass with the Benelli semi-automatic shotgun he kept on hand for just such an occasion. Duncan Schenck was not a big guy, but he didn't need to be. He was in his late fifties with a deep, permanent tan and a skinny frame that was just starting to go a little paunchy in the middle from too much of his own greasy cooking. Sharp gray eyes behind wire-rimmed glasses and a thin, salt-and-pepper ponytail. Duncan was ex-military and often referred to as a gun nut, although he told me he preferred the term "firearms enthusiast." I'd been fucking him for nearly two weeks, so I knew just how enthusiastic Duncan really was. There were more munitions in the concrete bunker under his old '63 Airstream trailer than out at the nearby Yuma Proving Grounds.

"Get down, Julie," he said, voice as calm as if he were calling an order up.

For a few near-fatal seconds that name "Julie" didn't mean anything to me. I'd had too many different names in the past month and seeing Thick Vic again had thrown me, made me forget all about my latest half-assed identity.

"Now," Duncan added and that was enough.

I flung the coffee carafe away and dropped down behind the counter as Duncan let loose with the shotgun. The sound of it was so loud I felt like I'd been hit by an auditory truck. The damp black rubber mat beneath my cheek smelled of ammonia and old food. There was a wilted piece of lettuce a few inches from my nose. I heard more shots above me and some shouting that sounded like Charlie Brown's teacher in my tortured, ringing ears, but I had no idea what was actually happening. I covered my head with my hands, sick from adrenaline and furious that this was happening now, when I had been so close to getting what I needed out of Duncan.

There was a crash, stagger and thump and when I uncovered my head, I saw that Vic and his kid were behind the counter with me. The kid had Vic's arm thrown over his shoulder and the two of them were wedged back against a stack of paper napkins. Vic was alive, but not happy about it. The kid was hyperventilating with too much white around the pretty golden-green irises of his eyes. After a long quiet minute, I risked a peek up over the counter. It didn't look good. The tall awkward Mexican kid was sprawled on the linoleum in a spreading ocean of blood. He was dead or might as well have been. Duncan was hanging over the lip of the pass, also dead or might as well have been. The old man with the pie was dead too, but from my vantage point it was hard to tell if he'd been shot or just keeled over with a grabber from all the excitement. The short, aggro kid was having a tense, hissed-between-clenched-teeth argument with the original shooter, who was shaking his head vehemently, cradling an obviously broken arm and saying the same thing over and over.

I noticed that the cheap Coca-Cola clock had fallen off the wall and landed face up a foot to my left. It was quarter after eleven. That meant the headlights I could see sweeping across the lot belonged to Highway Patrol Officer Norman Ketlin, who would be stopping in to refill his big thermal coffee cup one more time just like he did at eleven fifteen every other night of the week.

Norm didn't mess around. He didn't say, *"Freeze! Police!"* or anything like that, he just left the engine running and came out shooting. I grabbed my go-bag from under the counter and slung it over one shoulder. If I had a chance to get gone, this was it. Then I looked back at Vic and his kid.

The kid must've hit a mental wall. His handsome face was pale and blank with shock. If he had been conceived a few weeks earlier, he could have been my son. And Vic, that charming bastard, I'd already let him fuck up my life once. It would have been smarter to leave them, but I didn't. I couldn't.

"Come on," I whispered to the kid, throwing Vic's other arm over my own shoulder and indicating the swinging door to the kitchen. "Help me get him out of here."

The kid turned to me, eyes still way too big.

"They shot him," he said, or something along those lines. My hearing was still pretty iffy at this point. He could have meant any number of our patrons or employees, but I figured he meant Vic.

"They're probably gonna shoot us too if we don't get the hell out of here now," I said.

"Um, yeah okay," the kid replied.

Vic was still pretty skinny, but every pound hung limp and useless, dead weight between the two of us. I tried to keep Vic's head low as we duck-walked towards the kitchen door. More shots and furious Spanglish and I could hear Norm's deep, angry voice swearing, but didn't want to stick around to watch the show. More importantly, I didn't want to answer to anyone official. I had two shitty fake IDs and a halfway decent one, none of which would hold up to serious scrutiny.

When we got into the kitchen, we moved low and quiet past Duncan's body and the bloody, sizzling grill. Hannibal, our ex-con dishwasher, had cut and run the second the trouble started, leaving the back door wide open. He had the right idea.

"Where's your car?" I asked the kid, once we were outside.

He looked at me with a dangerously unfocused glaze in his eyes.

"Car!" I said as loudly as I dared. "Do you have one?"

The kid seemed to sharpen up a little and shook his head.

"I've got my bike," he said, indicating with his head. "Around front."

I remembered the tough-guy motorcycle helmet I'd seen on the table back in the diner. A motorcycle just wasn't gonna work. I didn't relish the idea of going back into the kitchen to get the keys to Duncan's truck out of his hip pocket but couldn't think of any other option until Vic spoke up.

"Angel," he said. "…my car…"

"Where are the keys?" I asked. "In your jacket?"

"Yeah," Vic said. "Brown '75 Bonneville."

As we headed around the side of the diner, the action tumbled out the kitchen door behind us. First the two Mexican kids, the short, aggro blond ducking behind the dumpster and the shooter with the broken arm making a run for Duncan's trailer. Norm came out fast on the shooter's heels as the kid zigzagged like a bunny across the dusty lot and dove under the trailer.

I'm not exactly sure what came next because it all happened so fast, but from my angle it looked like the bleach-blond kid popped up from behind the dumpster and took a shot at Norm just as he was bending down to grab the shooter's ankle and haul him out of his hiding place. The bullet must have missed Norm by an inch and hit the large propane tank on the side of Duncan's trailer. The subsequent series of explosions knocked us all to the ground and knocked any more wondering right out of my head.

When I looked up again I saw two people on fire. One was running in a wobbly, decaying circle and the other lying face down in the dust. It was impossible to tell who was who under the flames.

By the time I was able to look away, the kid had gotten his feet under him and lifted Vic across his shoulders in a fireman's carry. I got up off my skinned knees and ran for the parking lot, motioning for the kid to follow.

Out front was Norm's prowler, an aging green Town Car, a souped-up riceburner and Vic's beater Bonneville. At the far end of the lot was a candy apple Harley Shovelhead that sparkled like it had just rolled out of the showroom.

We made it to the Bonneville and the kid let Vic down beside the car, but Vic's legs wouldn't support his weight. He was still bleeding profusely, but his face was eerily calm.

"I can't…" Vic said. "You'd better…"

The kid held him up under the armpits while I went through his pockets. Gum. Change. Phone. A matchbook from a strip club. A pen featuring a sexy pin-up girl whose bikini disappeared if held at a certain angle. A folded printout of Google directions to the diner from Los Angeles. Finally, keys.

I unlocked the car, opened the passenger-side back door and then went around front and got behind the wheel. The engine coughed and spluttered as I fired it up and put it in gear. The kid laid Vic out in the back seat and then turned away, leaving the door open.

"I'll be right back," he said over his shoulder, heading across the lot towards his motorcycle.

I swore softly, gripping the wheel. There was a powerful stench of blood, bile and fresh shit inside the confined space of the car. The kid was fucking around with the fancy saddlebags on his bike and my foot was itching to hit the gas. I didn't. I waited.

"Talk to me, Vic," I said, tilting the rearview so I could see his pallid, sweating face. "You're not dead, are you?"

"You wish," he replied with ghost of a smirk on his bluish lips.

That's when the blond Mexican guy came around the corner of the diner and started shooting.

3.

Vic's kid saw the angry blond with the gun and ducked down behind his bike. He grabbed a saddlebag and made a sprint for the Bonneville while the blond emptied his magazine into the side of the car. God bless old-school American steel. If we'd been in a Kia, that would have been the end of it right there.

"Come on!" I called, gunning the engine.

The kid dove in the back and I floored the gas pedal, wheels spitting gravel and dust. Momentum slammed the door as I tore out of the lot. The blond jumped into the riceburner and fired it up, hot on our heels.

"Shit!" the kid said, looking out the back window. "Shit, he's following us. What are we gonna do?"

That was a good question. What the hell were we going to do? Or more specifically, what was I going to do?

The riceburner was gaining on us and the Bonneville was in pretty sorry shape, the indisputable tortoise in this particular race. It complained noisily as I bullied it up into the low eighties. There was a faded old sweatshirt on the passenger seat and I scooped it up and tossed it over my shoulder into the back.

"Use this to put pressure on the wound," I said. "You need to try and stop the bleeding."

"He's bleeding from the front and the back," the kid said, his voice pinched and breaking. "It smells really bad."

"Just do what you can," I said.

"Turn," the kid shouted. "Here, on the left!"

I did as he ordered, fishtailing wildly and taking out a small church billboard in the process.

"Watch it!" he said. "You're knocking him around back here."

"Look, you want to drive?" I asked, more than half serious. I've never been a car chase kind of girl. I've got other talents.

The turn put us on a long dark road through endless fields and farmland. Born and bred urbanite that I am, I never could get used to all that deep desert blackness. L.A. is never really dark at night. Neither is Chicago, where I grew up. Yuma is like the dark side of the moon. It spooked me a little, even when I didn't have an armed and jacked-up teenage killer trying to run me off the road.

"He's puking," the kid cried from the back seat. "He's puking! Jesus fuck!"

"Turn his head to the side," I said, flashing back to scraping a shitfaced and spewing Vic up off the sidewalk outside Gazarri's. "Don't let him choke."

When the riceburner rear-ended me, I just about had a heart attack. The hit sounded louder than the shotgun and my forehead bounced off the steering wheel, scattering flaming pinwheels across my vision. I'm sure there were seatbelts somewhere in that old Buick, but I hadn't bothered to look before I peeled out of the diner lot. I would have tried to find one then, but my hands were locked, white-knuckled, around the wheel.

Vic's kid was in the back freaking out, saying "fuck" a lot and being generally unhelpful. Vic had gone silent and could have been dead by then for all I knew. I had no idea where I was or which direction we were headed. With everything that I'd been through in the last few years, I had pretty much come to terms with the possibility of violent death, but this was different. It wasn't just me in the car.

The ricer hit again from the rear, more to the left this time, sending the Bonneville skidding off to the right. I wrestled the wheel, fighting to keep the old beast steady on the road, but the ricer came up close on the outside until we were neck and neck. I could see the blond in the driver's seat, gun raised and trying to steady his aim while driving with one hand. His eye was on me, not the road.

I wrenched the wheel to the left as hard as I could, the Bonneville chewing fiberglass as the shiny little ricer crumpled like a tissue box. The blond's shot shattered the driver's side window and buried itself in the foam padding of my seatback.

The wind through the broken window whipped my hair into my eyes, making it even harder to see the dark road. Behind me, the ricer swerved across the shoulder, flattening a barbed wire fence and several rows of lettuce, plowing up a fountain of loose dirt and eventually bumping to a crooked stop. The cockeyed headlights quickly receded in the Bonneville's rearview.

Silence in the backseat as I took the next two turns at random. A right then a left. I still had no idea where I was and was about to ask when Vic's kid spoke up between clenched teeth.

"Pull over."

"What?" I frowned into the rearview.

"I said pull over!"

I pulled over and Vic's kid tumbled out the door, tore off his bloody t-shirt like it was soaked in poison and then staggered away into the dry, tangled cotton field by the side of the road. I could hear the sound of vomiting. My hands were shaking as I peeled them off the wheel.

"Hey Vic," I said.

"Yeah?"

I looked into the rearview but couldn't see him. He must have been lying flat on the back seat.

"How you doing?"

"Well, you know…I've been feeling a little depressed lately," he said. "What with the recession and global warming and all that. Thanks for asking."

I laughed before I could stop myself. Son of a bitch always knew how to make me laugh.

"Come on, seriously."

"Well the good news is…I don't feel any pain," he said. "Bad news…I don't feel anything at all from the nipples down. That's really bad, isn't it?"

"It's not good," I said. "We need to get you to a hospital."

"Angel," he said. "Could you…come back here…for a minute?"

I didn't want to, but I did. In the back seat, the stench was even worse. The vinyl seat was sticky with coagulating blood and other pungent fluids. I had to move Vic's head so I could slide my legs in underneath it and that movement started the crater in his belly oozing again, something dark and foul that wasn't just blood. It took everything I had to try and keep my expression neutral.

"Sorry about the smell," Vic said, trying for a smirk that came out more like a grimace. He paused, and I could see how scared he was underneath the wisecracks. He took my hand in his. His fingers were damp and cold.

"Do you know those guys? The guy that shot you?" I asked.

Vic shook his head.

"Never seen them before."

"They seemed pretty high strung," I said. "Meth, maybe?"

"Coke," Vic replied. "Not crank. I oughta know. But hey, I pissed off a lot of people in my twenty-year career as a professional fuck-up, so I suppose those kids could be connected to any number of disgruntled former business associates. Or not."

"But why come after you in a public diner?" I asked. "Why not wait till you were alone?"

"You know…I hate to interrupt your sleuthing, Nancy Fuckin' Drew, but I'm on a ticking clock here," Vic said. "And there's really no way to say what I have to say so it don't sound all sappy and cliché. So fuck it, I'm just gonna say it. I'm sorry Angel. For being a lousy boyfriend, for…everything I put you through."

"It's okay," I said, wishing I could think of something that didn't sound so empty. It's hard to make words like "it's okay" mean anything when you're covered in blood and shit, miles from the nearest hospital.

"This isn't some bullshit twelve-step lip service either. I mean it," he said. "You were the only one that ever mattered. I just…"

He trailed off and I could feel all the muscles in my neck and shoulders go tense and stiff with anxious anticipation.

Vic may have driven me crazy a million different ways while we were together, but he understood me better than almost anyone. I knew he hadn't forgotten how uncomfortable any kind of mushy love talk makes me feel. The truth is, I can take on six strangers at once without batting an eye, but as soon as someone starts making love noises at me, I start looking for the exit.

There was an endless minute of heavy, loaded silence that felt as stifling and unbearable as the stench inside the car, then:

"Look, I know I got no right asking for favors," Vic said.

I squeezed his hand.

"Then don't," I said.

"Christ, Angel, you're still such a hard ass." Another grimace. "Come on, one last favor…for a dying man."

"You're not dying, for Christ's sake," I said. "And if you think I'm still gonna blow you after you shit your pants, you're out of your fucking mind."

He laughed, a soft, breathless wheeze.

"Nah. It'd be a waste of your legendary talent, since I wouldn't be able to feel it anyway."

That had started off as another wisecrack, but by the end of the sentence I could see the truth of those words starting to sink in. Again, the flash of raw fear in his eyes.

"Listen," he said. "I'm in bad shape here. Even if I do make it…well…." His grip on my hand was weak and getting weaker. "Just make sure the kid is okay."

"Oh, no," I said. "You fucker, don't lay this on me. You're gonna make it. You have to, you hear me?"

"Just promise me, Angel," he said. "Don't let anything

happen to him. Lie if you have to, but make it sound good, willya? Please? I'm dying here."

"Fine," I said. "Fine, I promise, but don't you fucking die on me."

But of course he did, the selfish prick.

I got out of the car and looked up at the cold stars. The sky seemed way too big and the headlights were the only illumination. I wrapped my arms around my body and let out a long shaky breath. I thought about the last time I was out in the desert with a dead man. I felt like I ought to cry or something, but it was as if I'd forgotten how.

I tried to remember what it was like the last time I'd cried. To remember the person I had been back then, beaten and terrified and wailing at the unfairness of it all. The shit I'd had to do to become the person that I was now, all those things conspired to wall up any hope of tears.

But goddamn, it had felt good to look into someone's eyes and have them really see me. Really know me, not just some generic, forgettable name on a fake ID. So much for that.

Truth was, I was furious at Vic for slipping so easily between the plates of my emotional armor. For making me care about him again, just in time to make me feel this.

"Sorry," the kid said when he returned to the car, wiping his mouth with his knuckles. "I just…"

He gave a little self-deprecating smirk and shrug that reminded me so much of Thick Vic I couldn't look at him.

"No problem, kid," I said.

He must have seen something in my expression or body language that clued him in. "What's wrong?" he asked, voice tightening with panic. "Is it my dad?"

"He's dead," I said. "I'm sorry."

The kid flipped out. Put his fist through the passenger side window. Screamed at the sky. Flailed and tripped and collapsed to his knees, flinging handfuls of dirt and pebbles around. I knew I should try to do something to comfort him, but I felt numb and frozen, crushed beneath the weight of my promise to Vic. I wanted to run as fast and as far as I could and never look back.

Eventually the kid tired himself out. I walked slowly over to where he was huddled on the shoulder.

"Let me see your hand," I said.

He held it out like a child with a boo-boo. I took his hand in both of mine and found that it was unexpectedly broad and massive, big enough to palm a paperback the way a magician would palm a playing card. Vic had big hands, but this kid's mitt was so huge that holding it made me feel like a little girl holding Daddy's hand to cross the street. The first two knuckles were crowned with old scabs and scars in addition to the fresh cuts from the safety glass. Surprisingly, the damage wasn't all that bad. Superficial, mostly. Kid had a fist like a cement block.

"What are we gonna do?" he asked.

"I don't know," I said, letting his hand drop.

The kid was shirtless and must have been freezing in the chilly desert night but he didn't show it. He had shaved off what little hair he might have had on his lanky torso and had the word "OUTLAW" tattooed in clichéd Old English lettering forming an arc over the tight six-pack of his belly. I could see little rims of fresh black scab still clinging to the edges of the O and the W. Again I was hit with a strange unfocused ache that might have been about Vic or a weird kind of disconnected loneliness or maybe something else entirely.

"You need to call the cops," I said.

There was no way around it now. Of course, I couldn't be anywhere near this mess when they arrived and it was a long, dark walk to anywhere, but I just didn't see any other option. I'd promised Vic I would make sure the kid was safe. In spite of my longstanding distrust of cops, getting him into the hands of the proper authorities was the only way I could think of to do that.

"My phone's in my jacket," he said. "Back at the diner."

I looked over my shoulder at the Bonneville. Of course I didn't have a phone. But Vic did.

"Wait here," I said.

I walked over to the car and stood for a moment by the back door, steeling myself. It didn't help. I hadn't thought the smell could possibly get worse, but it had.

I nearly threw up. Twice. The phone was in the pocket on the side of Vic's body with the fist-sized exit wound. There was a bright, ugly kind of hysteria lurking around the edges of my cool, but I managed to keep it submerged as I wiped the worst of the gore off the cheap little phone and flipped it open.

After all that, it didn't work. The little screen stayed gray and dead no matter what buttons I pushed. In a fit of blind fury, I flung the phone away into the cotton. The moment it left my hand, it occurred to me that maybe it just needed to be charged. Maybe Vic had one of those cords that plug into the cigarette lighter in the car. Too fucking late for that.

I got my backpack and the kid's saddlebag out of the car

and walked back over to where the kid stood with his back to me, scuffing the dirt with the toe of his boot.

"Is there somewhere that we could go?" I asked. "Somewhere with a phone?"

"Sure," he said. "My friend Hank lives about a mile down the road." He pointed. "That way."

"Well then, I guess we'd better start walking," I said.

"We can't just..." He looked back at the car. "...leave him."

"We'll call someone to pick him up as soon as we get to your friend's house."

He ran a shaking hand over his head.

"Right, okay."

"Let's go," I said, handing him his saddlebag.

He hefted it awkwardly, then unbuckled the flap and pulled out a notebook. He let the bag drop to the ground and started walking away.

When he noticed I wasn't following, he looked back. I was staring at the discarded bag. This was what he'd run back for—risked his life for—and now he was just throwing it away? "I only wanted this," he said, lifting the notebook. "It's stuff that I've been writing, you know, about my training and my feelings and stuff. I really didn't want to lose it. But I don't need the rest of this crap, and there's no point lugging the stupid bag around."

An unmarked disc in a plain paper sleeve—a CD? a DVD?—slipped out from between the pages of the notebook. Before it could fall to the ground, he caught it with his other hand. Not quite catching a fly with chopsticks, but still pretty impressive reflexes. He stuck the disc back in the book and handed it to me.

"Could you put it in your backpack? I can carry the backpack for you if you want."

"That's okay, kid," I said, sliding the notebook into a side pocket and wrapping my fingers tightly around the strap. "I got it." I didn't want to tell him that I couldn't stand the thought of someone else taking my go-bag. "We'd better get moving."

4.

I suppose you're wondering what I was doing waiting tables in a crummy little diner on a desert highway outside Yuma, Arizona. Maybe you read the coverage of that high-profile human trafficking trial I was mixed up in and figured anybody stupid enough to testify against people like that probably got WitSec'd away into anonymous oblivion. You'd be partially right, only of course it wasn't that simple.

Most of the nineteen months I spent in Witness Protection aren't even worth mentioning. It was lonely. I got set up in this grim, gray New England town where I didn't know anyone and didn't care. I was afraid to decorate my depressing apartment, because I didn't want to start to feel good about it, only to have it taken away like everything else that mattered. I missed my little house in the Valley. I missed my friends. I felt like a ghost, just going through the motions. Doing time inside my head between trips to the L.A. County courthouse.

When you go into WitSec, they tell you not to talk about the trial, or the events that led up to the trial, to anyone you meet in the aftermath. To tell the truth, it wasn't hard. I don't like to talk about it. I'd rather just move on and forget it ever happened.

Unfortunately, part of the deal with WitSec was seeing a therapist who knew the real score. Even though I wasn't allowed to talk to random people I met, I was expected to spill my guts to this shrink. It was supposed to help me adjust to my new life and cope with all the trauma I'd been through. It wasn't optional. The shrink's name was Lindsey and she looked like an Italian Greyhound with glasses. I disliked her right from the first session.

She was always making these unequivocal statements about "women in my situation" that had nothing to do with how I actually felt. She also insisted that I was in denial about my "abuse" in the adult film industry. I could never talk to her about the things that were really on my mind. About the fact I didn't feel like a poor violated victim at all. I felt like some kind of war veteran. Like I'd been forced to turn off something important inside me to become the killer I needed to be and I didn't have any idea how to turn it back on again. To become an ordinary civilian again, if such a thing were even possible. So instead I spent most of our time during the sessions fucking with her by telling the raunchiest, kinkiest stories about my "abuse." I think she secretly got off on it. Poor Lindsey just needed a decent orgasm.

Lindsey's office was in this quaint little house in the touristy section of town. At some point in the early '90s, the town council had voted to revitalize the area in order to attract more summer tourists. By revitalize they meant put in a Cheesecake Factory and a few shops that sold candles, ships in bottles and jewelry shaped like lobsters. They also converted a few of the old saltbox houses into cutesy office space for massage therapists, Pilates instructors and Lindsey.

It was our regular Tuesday appointment. I had just finished my workout and hadn't showered, as usual. I always made sure to do extra cardio on the days I met with Lindsey because it made her so obviously uncomfortable when I showed up all sweaty. Come to think of it, I'm pretty sure that Lindsey was appalled by every physical function of the human body.

I parked my crummy green Taurus in the small lot behind Lindsey's office and got out of the car. I was a few minutes early, and dawdled on the way up. It was a postcard kind of day. Late summer. Blue sky. I wasn't thinking about much of anything.

I walked up the stairs on autopilot. I'd tried so hard to stay sharp, stay wary, but the same old same old makes you soft. I would have just walked right in and that would have been that, but my sneaker had come untied on the stairs and I paused to tie it in front of Lindsey's door. That's when I heard a horribly familiar voice coming from inside her office. A voice I was sure I'd never hear again.

"Where is she?"

When I heard that distinctive high-pitched Croatian accent through the closed door, I thought for a second that I *had* gone nuts, that all the abuse Lindsey kept going on and on about had finally caught up to me and pushed me off the deep end. Austin, the WitSec marshal in charge of my case, had assured me a thousand times that no one had ever been able to find and kill a protected witness in the history of the organization. The only way witnesses ever got killed was if they broke the rules and contacted someone from their old life. Everyone I cared about was already dead, so there was no temptation there for me. So what the fuck was going on? How could they have found me? After I'd endured endless months of this lonely gray town where everyone was white and sour and disapproving, the bastards had found me anyway. I might as well have stayed in L.A., where at least I could get decent *tacos al pastor*.

There was no doubt in my mind that they had poor skinny, joyless Lindsey tied up in her immaculate, environmentally friendly and allergen-free office. If they weren't torturing her yet, they'd start soon. They'd make her tell them everything. In retrospect, I still feel kinda bad about that. She was a pain in my ass, but nobody deserves that kind of action.

I backed silently away from the door. Fear and rage were duking it out in my head and there was a scary moment when the rage almost won. I almost charged through the door and attacked that weaselly motherfucker with my bare hands. I knew it was stupid, fatally stupid, but there was this quiet, compelling voice in my head telling me it would be better to die with my hands around that bastard's neck than to live on the run, always afraid. I have to admit, I still hear that voice sometimes, even now.

But, of course, I didn't charge in there like some action heroine out of a movie. I ran.

5.

Vic's kid and I walked along the side of the dark desert road. He had a miniature flashlight on his keychain that sent out a tiny circle of bluish light. It only made the dark around us seem darker.

"What's your name?" I asked.

"Cody," he said.

"Cody what?" It probably wasn't Ventura, or Pagliuca either, for that matter. Pagliuca was Vic's real last name. I had no idea what Skye West's real name was.

"Noon," the kid said. "Cody Noon."

I was thinking about what I was gonna say when he asked my name, but he beat me to the punch.

"My dad called you Angel," he said. "You're not…" He chewed his lip, eyes on his boots. "Don't take this the wrong way or anything, but…are you a porn star?"

I didn't answer, but he wouldn't let it go.

"You are," he said. "You're Angel Dare, aren't you?"

What the hell was I supposed to tell him? There was no point denying it. I nodded, hating how raw and vulnerable I felt under that huge black sky.

"I knew it," he said. "Wow. You look so different. I never would have recognized you."

"That's just because I have clothes on."

He laughed, then looked away. It seemed like he had

43

something else he wanted to say, but whatever it was, he kept his mouth shut.

We walked in silence for a few minutes. I could see he was starting to shiver, but trying to be a man about it. The quarter moon ducked in and out from behind swift-moving cloud banks. There was a small strip mall up ahead with no open businesses. On the other side of the road was a lot dealing in tractors and heavy farm equipment, also closed. There was a big dog in the farm equipment dealer's fenced yard, a scrappy brown mutt that eyed us suspiciously but didn't bark.

As we walked, the tight, nauseous dread in the pit of my stomach seemed to get worse rather than better. I was itching to get out of town. To be anywhere but Yuma.

After another twenty minutes of tense, awkward silence, we arrived at our apparent destination, a sorry little yellow house in dire need of fresh paint and a new roof. Or a can of kerosene and a match. The cheerful metal welcome sign out front was faded and rusty around the edges and featured a friendly, waving cartoon animal of indeterminate species that had been shot through the left eye with a small caliber rifle.

Cody led the way up the dusty driveway and laid into the flimsy door with both fists.

"Hank!" he called. "Come on, Hank, open up!"

The sudden racket made my skin crawl, even though there were no other houses in sight. After what seemed like an hour, the door finally opened, revealing a man in his underwear.

Even when I'm up to my eyeballs in paranoia, running from doped-up killers in the middle of the night, there are some things that will never escape my notice. A body like that guy's is one of those things.

He was just a few inches taller than me, with a compact but hard and powerful build. A build like that wasn't just for show. A build like that meant business. He had broad shoulders with a large, crescent-shaped surgical scar on the right. Strong arms and thick, muscular thighs. He hadn't bothered to shave the hair off his chest and belly like Cody had. His tighty-whiteys had been scrubbed so many times that they were worn thin, nearly see-through. I liked what I could see through them. When my gaze finally made it up to his face, I was more than a little disappointed.

He had a face that looked like something the tribe who made those stone heads on Easter Island might have come up with if they'd attempted a portrait of Chuck Norris. His large nose had been repeatedly smashed and flattened. His eyes were so pale they were barely blue and he had an equal length of blond stubble on his head and his heavy jaw. His crooked ears were cauliflowered, puffy and swollen up like they had hemorrhoids, the right more so than the left.

"Dammit, Cody," he said. "You got any fuckin' idea…" He looked over Cody's shoulder at me, then dipped his chin, shifting his gaze to his bare feet. "Scuze me, ma'am. I didn't realize Cody'd brought company."

His voice was deep, distinctly Southern and full of gravel. I had the feeling if he'd been wearing a hat, he would have taken it off.

There was a beat of awkward silence before he seemed to realize he was in nothing but skivvies. He blushed and began to stammer, then slammed the door.

"Just give me a minute, willya?" he finally managed to say through the closed door.

When he opened the door again, he was dressed in black track pants and a t-shirt advertising some kind of muscle-building supplement.

"Why didn't you say you brought company," he said to Cody. "Well, ain't you gonna introduce me?"

"Angel," Cody said distractedly. "This is Hank 'The Hammer' Hammond."

I cringed, wishing I'd thought to ask him not to use the name Angel.

"Just Hank'll do," Hank said with a kid's big guileless grin. He seemed to have completely forgotten about his previous embarrassment.

He put out a thick, calloused hand that was stiff and permanently curled as if never more than two inches from a fist. I shook it. It felt like an inanimate object.

"Charmed," I said, looking back over my shoulder. "But I really think we ought to go inside."

"Sure, you bet," Hank said, standing aside. "Come on in."

Inside the little house, it was cramped and cluttered. The ugly brown and orange furniture looked as if it had been preserved in amber since 1974. There were a lot of magazines lying around and at first glance I thought they were gay porn. When I looked closer, I realized the half-naked men were fighting, not fucking. I recognized that big side of beef who'd knocked up Jenna Jameson and then allegedly knocked her around. In addition to the magazines, there were also a lot of scattered fight DVDs, dirty Tupperware containers, big plastic cups crusted with the dried-up remnants of protein shakes and a distressing number of empty orange prescription pill bottles. Hank was gathering up armloads of junk and dumping it all randomly into drawers and cabinets.

"I'd've straightened up if I knew…"

He paused and turned towards Cody, who stood in the center of the room with his fists clenched and shoulders shaking. He was fighting not to cry and losing. I looked down at the stained carpet, feeling nervous and uncomfortable. I felt bad for the kid but there wasn't anything I could do about it. I couldn't even figure out how I was supposed to feel about what had happened to Thick Vic.

"Hey, what's all this about?" Hank asked, coming forward and slinging a huge, protective arm around Cody.

"Fucking bastards," Cody stammered, his face crimson. "They… They…"

"Come on now," Hank scolded softly, steering Cody over to the lumpy sofa. "You oughta watch your mouth in front of a lady."

The idea of anyone watching their mouth around me was pretty hilarious. Guess Hank never saw my scene in *Trash Talking Tramps*. Still, I have to admit it was kind of charming.

He sat Cody down on the couch like a child with a skinned knee, surprisingly mother hen-ish for such an ugly brute.

"Why don't you just sit still for a minute and take some deep breaths. Come on now, breathe. There you go."

"They killed my dad," Cody said all in a rush. "I just barely met him and they killed him. They tried to kill me too, but…"

"Tried to kill you?" Hank said, frowning. "Who tried to kill you?"

"I had the guy who did it, but I let him go," Cody said, standing up and shaking off Hank's comforting hand. "I had him, broke his fucking arm for him too, but when the shooting started, I…I got scared. I got scared and fucking let him go. Fuck!"

He flipped the cluttered coffee table up on its side, kicked it across the room and then took a wild swing at the wall, but Hank was on him in a heartbeat, holding him tight from behind and talking to him in low soothing tones. Cody fought against him at first, but eventually whatever Hank was saying started working and the kid nodded, sniffling and settling down.

"Okay now," Hank said, guiding Cody back to the sofa. Hank fumbled around with various pill bottles until he found one that wasn't empty and dumped a pair of tiny blue tablets into Cody's hand. "Ain't no point second-guessing your fight after the bell's already rung. All you can do is work on being better next time. So why don't you just relax for a little while and we can talk more about this later. I got the pay-per-view there on the Tivo. You wanna watch a little bit? Your boy Kenner sure was something in the main."

Cody nodded and dry swallowed the pills. Hank set the coffee table back on its feet, put on the television and began messing around with several remotes. When he got the program he wanted to start playing, he put the remotes on the coffee table where Cody could reach them.

"Listen, Hank," I said softly. "You need to call the cops." I looked back at Cody. "And I can't be here when they arrive."

"Well," Hank said. "Whatever issues you might have with the law are none of my business. But I can tell you right now there might be a problem or two with this plan of yours."

"What do you mean?"

"Well for starters," he said. "Ain't got no phone service at the moment, on account of I forgot to pay the bill again."

"Then you could give him a ride to the station."

"No can do," Hank replied. "Ain't supposed to drive no more on account of my migraine headaches. Anyway, look at him." He gestured towards Cody, already curled up and snoring on the couch. "Boy's out cold. He ain't going nowhere tonight. Not after what I gave him."

"Do you have a car?" I asked.

"Got my old truck out back," he said. "Reckon it still runs."

"Then he can drive there himself in the morning," I said. "Look, I promised I'd get him somewhere safe and here he is, so if I could just get cleaned up and out of this uniform, I'll hit the road and be out of your hair."

"You planning on going off alone on foot in the middle of the night?" he asked. He bent down over the sleeping boy and pulled Cody's boots off his feet. "Ain't nothing around for miles. Nothing that'd be open this time of the night, anyways." He shook his head. "No, ma'am, I can't let you do that. Ain't safe."

"I can take care of myself," I said.

"I don't doubt that for a minute," he replied, setting the boots on the floor and tossing a ratty knitted blanket over Cody. "But just the same, I think you'd better stay put till sunup. Cody can drop you at the Greyhound station first thing."

He was right. I was exhausted, shaken and in no shape for hiking. Or arguing.

"Can I get you a cold drink?" he asked. "What'd you say your name was again?"

"Angel," I said, too exhausted to lie. "And yeah, that'd be great, thanks."

"Ain't got nothing but diet, so I hope that'll do. I'm trying to cut weight."

"That's fine," I said, wondering where he was planning on cutting weight from. He didn't have an ounce of fat on him.

I followed him into the tiny kitchen. He handed me a supermarket-brand diet cola from out of the disproportionately enormous fridge and then began bustling around, tidying up.

"Go ahead and take a load off." He motioned to a spindly aluminum chair with a torn vinyl cushion, the only one in the room. "I'm just gonna get this mess taken care of real quick. If I'da known company was coming I'da straightened up a bit."

He seemed flustered, repeating himself. I wanted it to be because of me, but it was hard to be sure.

He started methodically washing a teetering stack of identical square Tupperware containers. I popped open the cola and was sucking in the tart carbonated rush of air around the mouth of the can when I noticed a revolver sitting on the kitchen table. The cylinder was open and beside it was a single bullet standing upright on its flat end like a tiny hard-on. I was about to comment on that when Hank said, "You want to tell me what happened tonight?"

I sat down in the uncomfortable chair and filled him in. As I told the story, I started to think more and more about who those guys might have been. They didn't seem interested in robbing the place, not that there was anything obviously worth robbing in the diner. They could have been after Duncan's money or his guns—but if they'd known about the guns, they would have been much better prepared. On the other hand they were clearly coked up to eleven and even though Vic said he didn't know them, I couldn't rule out a connection with his drug dealing past. I shared some of these musings with Hank and he nodded his huge head, dunking another container into the suds.

"How long have you known Cody?" I asked to change the subject.

"Oh, around five years." He frowned and looked up at the low ceiling like the answer might be up there. "Well, more like three I guess. I forget exactly." He paused, then turned on the hot water in the sink. "About three years, I guess."

"What's he like?" I asked.

"Well, that boy's got a chin on him," Hank said. "Real heavy hands, hits like a Mack truck, but his stand up is still a little sloppy. His ground game ain't half bad though, on account of his varsity wrestling background. His main problem is he gets frustrated way too easy. If the fight don't go the way he wants in the first round he gets all bent out of shape mentally and starts making mistakes. But you see that there's just him being young. All that boy needs is a little growing up. The fight game's a tough racket, and I ain't just talking about the action inside the ring. Fight game can chew you up and spit you out the second you let your guard down. But with a good corner behind him, I think Cody's got a real shot at the big time."

I smiled and took another sip of my cheap pop. That guy sure could talk your ear off once you got him started, and

Cody was apparently one of his favorite topics. Unfortunately, I had absolutely no idea what anything he had just said actually meant.

"So Cody's a fighter?" I asked, hoping for a little more of an explanation.

Hank turned to me with a puzzled frown.

"Yeah," he said. "Ain't you?"

"I'm a lover, not a fighter," I said but as soon as it was out, I realized it wasn't exactly true anymore.

"I just figured," Hank said. "On account of the way you hold your body, like you're always ready for it. And that profile. You got a fighter's nose."

I never did get my nose fixed after it was broken. I guess you could say it was a fighter's nose and I couldn't help but take that as a compliment, coming from someone like Hank. But I could see it dawning very slowly on him that maybe there was another reason a woman might have a broken nose. He blushed again. There was something inexplicably sexy about seeing a tough guy like him blush so easily.

"I sure didn't mean…" He picked up a Tupperware container and started drying it off with a striped dish towel. His hands were shaking a little. "I didn't mean to bring up something that ain't none of my business." He looked down at his hands, then put the container away. "And I don't want to make it sound like you ain't pretty, because you are. I just don't think sometimes before I speak. Sometimes?" He shook his head. "Most of the time, I reckon."

"Forget it," I told him.

"Yes ma'am," Hank said, wiping his sudsy hands. "You wanna watch the fights?"

"Sure," I said.

We went into the living room and I stood for a moment looking at Thick Vic's kid. He was curled up on his side, conked out with the blanket more bunched up around him than covering him. Sleeping, he didn't look anything like his father. I wondered what the hell I was doing here.

Hank offered me the remaining easy chair but I shook my head and I sat on the scratchy carpet with my back against the sofa. Hank lowered himself slowly, stiffly into the chair, leaning towards the television with his elbows on his knees. We watched the fights.

Two guys were bashing the crap out of each other inside a fenced-in ring. Then they were down on the mat, rolling around together. One guy was cut above the eye, bleeding. The audience was filled with celebrities and girls who looked like they were in the business, but I didn't see Jenna. I tried to imagine Cody in there, fighting like that. I tried not to think about Vic.

I guess I nodded off, because I woke to Hank's big calloused hand shaking my shoulder.

"Hey," he said. "You fell asleep. Why don't you go lay down proper. You look like you could use some rest."

"What about you?" I asked when he led me into the bedroom and motioned towards the narrow single bed. "Where are you going to sleep?"

"I don't sleep all that much anymore," Hank said. "Seems like I spend most nights in my chair by the TV. You want a t-shirt or something to sleep in?"

"Sure," I said. "Thanks."

He handed me a folded-up black shirt from one of the

drawers in a rickety dresser and then made himself scarce without another word. I wiggled out of my scratchy polyester waitress uniform, took off my bra but not my panties and pulled the shirt over my head. It was huge on me and featured the badly designed logo of a martial arts school.

I stood there for a minute, looking around a strange man's bedroom. There was a small pile of dirty clothes in one corner. A cheap nightstand. More pill bottles. A modest stack of girlie magazines. The one on top was the latest *Hustler*. The exotic brunette on the cover was named Ruby Kahn and listed as "World Famous Asian Starlet of the Year." I didn't recognize her. Something about that fact made me feel a fleeting stab of lonely homesickness that was gone before I could get a handle on it.

It seemed pretty clear from the single bed and the fact that the smut was right out in the open that no women ever came into this room. I couldn't help wondering why not. After all, with a body like his, there ought to be plenty of lonely housewives and fight groupies willing to overlook his ugly mug. But I was too exhausted to wonder for long so I just staggered over to the bed and collapsed in a heap. The sheets were pretty clean for a bachelor's bed, with only the slightest hint of male sweat and unfamiliar cologne. I'd been sleeping in other people's beds so much lately that I barely even noticed.

6.

I woke to fists banging on the door. For several terrifying seconds, I had no idea where I was. I put it together in quick flashes. A man's bed, not Duncan's. The extra large men's t-shirt I was wearing. Hank. Cody. The shootout. It couldn't be anything but trouble at the door.

"Hank," a reedy male voice called. "You in there?"

I slipped into the living room and tiptoed over to the window beside the door. Cody was still out on the sofa, snoring softly. Hank was nowhere in sight. I peered out through the blinds and saw two men. Neither Mexican nor Croatian, but somehow that didn't make me feel any better. The guy doing the knocking was short, squat and white, a horny toad in a cowboy hat. The other was a huge, dead-eyed Native American whose neck was the same size as my waist.

Hank chose that moment to come jogging down the drive. He was wearing a strange silver plastic two-piece suit with tight, gathered wrists and ankles. He was so sweaty and red he looked like he had just stepped out of a hot shower. He slowed, limping slightly on his left leg and twisting his shoulders from side to side, then came to a stop and leaned against the porch railing, breathing heavily.

"What can I do for you boys?" he asked the two visitors, pulling off the plastic shirt and letting about a gallon of sweat pour out into the dust. Underneath the shirt was something that looked like a bulletproof vest with rows of narrow pockets holding flat metal weights.

The horny toad leaned close to Hank and spoke low, almost too low for me to hear.

"Trouble, Hank," he said. "Looks like your boy Cody fucked up big time."

"Fucked up how?" Hank asked with a worried frown.

"Never mind," the man said. "All you need to know is that Mr. Lovell would like a word with him." He looked at the door. "He's not here now, is he?"

I pulled back from the window, heart beating way too hard and mind desperately working the angles. Even if there were any place to hide, it wasn't like I could bodily drag Cody there without making any noise. I had my Sig in my backpack, plus a cute little compact Para Warthog, a gift from the late Duncan Schenk, and I was about to use one of them when I suddenly had a better idea. I pulled Hank's t-shirt over my head, tossed it on the floor and opened the door.

"Hey, baby," I said, standing there in the doorway in nothing but my thong panties. "You coming back to bed or what? Oh…!" I pretended to notice the two men and covered myself up with my arms, making sure to do a really lame job of it.

The horny toad took one look at my not-really-covered tits and started chuckling and elbowing his stoic buddy. Hank was staring at me dumbfounded with his mouth open. I hoped he wouldn't blow it.

"Hank, you dog," the horny toad said. "You just let us know if you see Cody, you hear?"

"Uh…will do," Hank said. He looked back at me. "Now if you boys'll excuse me."

The two men walked away shaking their heads and Hank came inside the house, locking the door behind him.

He stood for a moment inside, looking shyly down at his hands.

"I..." he said. "Maybe I oughta shower." He frowned, looked at me and then back down at his hands. He was already so red from jogging in the plastic suit, I didn't think it was possible for him to get any redder, but he managed. "I'm sorry, but ...we didn't really...last night ...I mean...did we...?"

"Not yet," I said with a wink and picked up his t-shirt off the floor, slipping it back over my head. "Trust me, honey, you don't forget a woman like me."

"Nah, of course not," he said with a relieved laugh, like he had been genuinely worried he might have somehow missed something. "Of course not."

"Who were those guys?" I asked.

He frowned. "Who?"

"Those guys just now," I said. "The ones looking for Cody. Who were they?"

"Oh yeah, right," Hank said. "Those are Mr. Lovell's boys. Mr. Lovell's the guy who co-owns the school where I teach. He books legit fights over at the Kikima Casino but he also runs some other, not-so-legit action south of the border." He looked over at Cody asleep on the sofa and paused for a second with the weighted vest half off. "I guess you'd better wake him up. Looks like we got us some trouble."

Hank headed off, presumably to shower, and I knelt down by the sofa to shake Cody awake. Nothing doing. The kid was dead to the world. I shook him harder and he rolled away from me, making an incoherent noise of protest.

"Cody," I said. "Get up. Come on now."

Eventually one bloodshot eye cracked open.

"Morning, gorgeous," he said, giving me a lascivious up and down. "How was I last night? I can't remember a thing."

"Look, we got trouble, kid," I said. "Some guy named Mr. Lovell sent a couple of guys looking for you."

He sat up and rubbed a palm over his stubbled scalp, face suddenly serious.

"Lovell? But I…"

Hank came out of the bathroom then. He was clean-shaven, wearing loose-fitting knee-length shorts and no shirt. It was hard not to stare.

"Y'all want some eggs?" he asked.

"Shouldn't we get Cody over to the police station?"

"Sure we will, but the kid's gotta eat. You should, too. I'll get some coffee going."

"Thanks, Hank," Cody said.

Cody went into the bathroom and I went into the kitchen. Hank was at the stove, his broad back to me.

"You want the yolks in or out?" he asked.

"I'll take it however you're giving it," I said, sitting down in the single chair. "Why do you think this guy Lovell would be after Cody?"

"Can't rightly say," he said, separating yolks from whites and dumping the whites into a sizzling pan. "But whatever it is, you can bet it's bad." He shook his head. "Take it from me, you don't want a guy like Mr. Lovell gunning for you."

Cody came into the kitchen, water beaded on his stubbled head.

"It wasn't my fault," he said. "Honest. It just happened."

Choke Hold

I arched an eyebrow at Hank. Hank split the enormous mound of scrambled egg whites among three paper plates and then pulled three identical Tupperware containers from the fridge. Each container held a single cooked chicken breast. He placed one plate on top of one of the containers and handed the stack to me, along with a plastic fork and knife. Then did the same for Cody, taking the last one for himself.

"Coffee'll be up in a minute," he said. "Y'all want hot sauce?"

Cody and I sat on the couch and Hank sat in the recliner. For a few minutes, we just ate. The cold chicken was plain, dry and flavorless, the egg whites bland as toilet paper. It took about a gallon of hot sauce for me to choke half the food down, but neither Cody or Hank seemed to care. They were just shoveling and chewing like machines refueling. Hank took a short break to bring out three paper cups of strong black coffee and a plastic shopping bag.

"All right, Cody," Hank said, pulling bottles of vitamins and herbal supplements from the bag and downing handful after handful. "I think you'd better start filling us in here."

"Look, I told you," Cody said around a mouthful of chicken, "It just happened. He said it was no big deal."

"What just happened?" I asked.

"You know I'm going to Vegas to be on *All American Fighter: The Next Generation*," Cody said. "Well, Hank knows. Matt Kenner came out to our school scouting talent for Team Kenner in the new season of *All American Fighter* where all the guys are supposed to be eighteen to twenty-one. Have you seen the show?"

I shook my head.

"It's these two teams. And all the team members have to live together in one big house with cameras rolling 24/7. They fight against the other team and guys get eliminated and the one guy who wins at the end gets an AAFC contract."

"Got it," I said.

"Of course you know Matt Kenner, right?"

I shrugged.

"He's only the current heavyweight champion in the AAFC," he said like I was from Mars or something. "He's a real cool guy too, and said I had the most potential out of all the students. Told me to be at his dojo in Vegas at 8 AM sharp this Sunday morning, that the filming for the show would be starting that day. There's no way I'm gonna miss an opportunity like that, right? This is my big chance. He gave me his card, see?"

Cody dug out his wallet and took out a business card, handing it to me. Kenner's name and the name and address of an MMA training camp in Vegas.

"Right," I said, handing the card back to him. "But what does that have to do with this Mr. Lovell?"

"I'm getting to that," Cody said, slipping the card back into his wallet. "I've been fighting for Mr. Lovell at Kikima for like four months, but I have a year contract. He gave me an advance and, well, I still owe him seven more fights. But I wouldn't be able to fight at Kikima while I was on *All American Fighter*, so I asked him if there was any way he could let me out of the contract early. He said sure, if I could pay back the money he gave me. Only I already spent it."

I was starting to see where this was going. My bland breakfast felt like a brick in my belly.

"Well, Mr. Lovell also books these other fights. In Mexico, no holds barred. All the students do it, so it's like no big deal. Anyway, Mr. Lovell wanted me to fight for him in Mexico." He looked over at Hank and then down at his feet. "He wanted me to throw the fight."

Hank stopped with another handful of vitamins halfway to his mouth. "What?"

"Well, what the hell was I supposed to do?" Cody asked. "I didn't have any other way to pay him back."

"But you won that fight," Hank said. "Knockout in the first round."

"That's the thing." Cody said. "I didn't mean to do it. I just caught the guy right on the button with that knee. He dropped right into it. It was like, an accident. I was supposed to submit in the third but that fucking knee... Anyway Lovell said he understood. He said I could do a rematch tonight and he'd make double. He said he understood and it was no big deal."

"Well I'd call sending a bunch of coked-up bangers to shoot you and your father a pretty big deal," Hank said.

Cody went pale.

"You think this is my fault?" he asked in a small voice.

"What do you mean?" I asked. "We have no proof it was Lovell that sent those guys."

"But he *might* have." Cody put down his plate on the cluttered coffee table and stood. "And if it *is* true, then it's my fault that my dad's dead. I should never have agreed to meet him. If he'd never met me, he'd still be alive. Fuck."

Even if it was true that Lovell was responsible for the shooting at the diner, Vic could have died a thousand other times during his crazy self-destructive life. I wanted to say this to Cody, but couldn't seem to form any words. I looked down into my empty coffee cup.

Hank stood.

"Now, just take it easy," he said.

"Fuck that!" Cody said, tensing like he was getting ready for another round of table throwing. That kid had apparently inherited Vic's Italian tantrum gene in spades. "I'm gonna kill him."

"Okay," I said. "Enough already. This isn't doing anybody any good. Now pull yourself together and let's get you down to the police station. You want them to catch whoever's behind all this, don't you?"

"It's Lovell," Cody said. "I fucking know it!"

"What'd I tell you about that kind of language?" Hank asked.

"Fine, look," I said. "Let's say it is Lovell. You want him to get arrested for what he did, don't you?"

Cody sat back down, nodded.

"You're the victim here, kid," I said. "You didn't do anything wrong. But you can't just go after this guy on your own."

Luckily, no one else in the room knew how laughably ironic those words sounded coming from me.

"You don't know me," Cody said. "You don't know anything about me or what I can do. And I'm not your fucking kid."

"Mind your mouth, son," Hank said, voice stern and serious. "I done told you once, I ain't gonna tell you again. I won't have no disrespect to women in this house."

"Sorry," Cody said, looking down and away.

"Look," I said. "Maybe you're not my kid, but you are

Vic's kid and before he died he asked me to take care of you, so that's exactly what I plan to do whether you like it or not. Now I'm gonna go get cleaned up and I want you to pull yourself together and be ready to go by the time I get out."

Hank busied himself clearing away the remnants of breakfast while Cody pouted and made a big show of putting on his boots. I grabbed my go-bag and headed into the john.

It was pretty grungy in there, but not appallingly so. Sad, cheap shower stall, glass cloudy and thickly scaled from hard water. Everything was wet, like Cody hadn't bothered to close the shower door. The only towel was soaked and crumpled up on the floor. My search for a fresh towel revealed lots of mentholated muscle rub, more fight magazines and even more pill bottles, if that were possible. Mostly meds for pain and inflammation, but also other stuff I'd never even heard of. Eventually I found a clean towel, shucked off Hank's t-shirt and slipped into the shower.

I had to wait on washing my hair, since there was no shampoo or conditioner anywhere in the bathroom. I pictured Hank washing his stubbled head with bar soap and smiled to myself. Then I started to picture the rest of him in the shower and had to kill that line of thinking if I wanted to get out of there any time soon.

I got out, dried off and slipped quickly into clean clothes from my go-bag. Comfortable, athletic clothes that were easy to run in. That's pretty much all I ever wore anymore. I figured I'd take the waitress uniform with me and toss it into a public trash barrel in another town, just to be on the safe side.

7.

When I came out of the bathroom, Hank had squeezed his thick torso into a skintight, long-sleeved black spandex shirt with the same bad logo that graced the t-shirt I'd worn the night before. He was lacing up his battered sneakers.

"Did you remember to take your Topamax?" Cody asked him.

"Oh yeah, right," Hank said, fumbling through a drawer and sorting through handfuls of pill bottles. "I'm pretty sure it's in here somewhere."

Cody picked up a bottle off the floor near the couch and tossed it to Hank.

"What about the Klonnopin?" Cody asked.

"I'd just as soon skip that one. At least till after class," Hank said. "I'm stupid enough without it."

"Well, bring it with you," Cody said. "Just in case."

"My momma's been dead for twenty-two years," Hank said, suddenly testy. "And I been getting along just fine without her, thank you very much."

Hank downed a couple of tablets from the bottle Cody gave him and followed them up with several more from various other bottles in the drawer.

"All right you two," I said. "Let's get on the road."

The three of us squeezed into Hank's old pickup. Cody drove. No one talked.

We dropped Hank off at the martial arts school first, since

he had classes to teach. The school was inside a long narrow storefront and through the big plate glass windows I could see pairs of young students practicing throwing each other down on the mat. Hank got out slow on stiff joints, then turned back and offered his bulky paw.

"It was a real pleasure to meet you," he said. "Even under the circumstances. Good luck out there, Angel."

I took his hand in both of mine, held onto it for a moment longer than I should have, then let it go.

"Take it easy, Hammer."

He flashed that big, child-like smile again and then shut the door and turned away.

Cody watched Hank walk over to the door of the school, then put the truck in gear.

"He's a legend, you know," Cody said. "One of the best. I never would have made it onto *All American Fighter* if not for him."

Cody waited for another, nearly identical truck to pass by, then pulled away from the curb.

"When I was growing up," he said, looking at the road, not at me, "I was pretty much on my own most of the time. Never had anybody to make sure I did my homework or brushed my teeth. My mom…she's got her own problems and my dad, well, you know about him. I was getting into fights all the time. Failing everything. Then I started training at Richland's and I met Hank."

"He seems like a real decent guy," I said.

"People love to talk all kinds of shit about him on the forums, that he's a loser and a has-been, and sure he's been through some rough times, but when he was at the top of his game, fighting in Japan, man, he was unbeatable. Pound for pound the most dangerous welterweight in the sport, no question. Better than Richland, even. So versatile, you never knew what he was gonna throw at you. You wanted to stand up, he'd knock you out so fast and so clean you'd be down before you even knew what hit you. You wanted to go to the ground, he'd play chess with you, give you a little slack just to see what you were made of and then when he got bored, he'd submit your ass without breaking a sweat. His title fight against Shinya Fujita was a fucking clinic. But you know, the fans here don't want to watch a master technician like Hank. They want a big showy brawler, throwing haymakers they can see from the cheap seats. That's why Hank never got a fair shake in this country."

Cody went on and on like that, and I just watched him talk. Not listening so much to his specific words as the intense passion behind them. He seemed to love the sport in general and Hank in particular. Hank had obviously stepped in to fill the daddy-shaped hole that Vic left behind while he was off being a fuck-up. I couldn't help but wonder, if Vic had lived, would he have stood a chance of filling Hank's sizable shoes?

"Don't be mad if I say this," Cody said in an abrupt conversational swerve, "but I saw you in some videos online. You and my dad at first, because I was trying to find out information about him, but then I saw you with some other guys too. I couldn't watch the ones with my dad in them. Even though I never really knew him, it was…I don't know. Just wrong. But you? You were awesome."

"Thanks," I said, smiling slightly and looking out the window.

"You were his girlfriend, huh?" Cody asked. "My dad, I mean. You know, before…"

"A long time ago."

"What was he like?"

Man, that was a loaded question. I felt swamped with a hundred vivid and painful memories, none of which were appropriate to share with Vic's teenaged son.

I remembered our first scene together, how Vic kept on whispering the most outrageous, hilarious things in my ear and cracking me up while I was trying to be all sexy and serious. I remembered our first time off camera, silent, slow and kissing the whole time, pressed so tightly together that there was no room for a shooter to get between us. I remembered Vic cranked out of his mind and screaming on my lawn at 4:30 in the morning, waking up all the neighbors. I remembered Vic strung out and weighing less than I did, looking like a hollow, wasted shell of who he used to be.

I didn't want to talk about Vic just in terms of the way he fucked, like Cody and Hank had talked about each other in terms of the way they fought. I also didn't want to talk about Vic just in terms of the way he'd fucked up.

"Well, he was real sharp and funny," I finally managed to say. "He always made everybody laugh and never took himself too seriously. He would do anything for his friends." I looked up at the big sky. "He was from Chicago originally, like me, so he never had that flaky shallow L.A. mentality that you get so often in the business."

"My mom hates him," Cody said quietly. "She never wanted me to meet him."

I nodded, said nothing. We drove.

"There's the station," Cody said, pulling up opposite a sleek modern building fronted by decorative desert foliage. "I'll jump out here, and you can take Hank's truck and leave it in the Greyhound lot. It's just a few blocks down First." He pointed through the bug-smeared windshield. "Make a left on 17th Place. That's 17th *Place*, not 17th Street. Leave the key under the mat and I'll pick the truck up later. It's not like anyone would want to steal this piece of shit."

"Right," I said, but couldn't say anything more, because I suddenly didn't want to let him go.

Not that I had a brilliant alternative suggestion or a better plan or anything. I just felt like he was my last connection to Vic and to my old life.

"Don't forget to watch me on *All American Fighter*!" he said.

I couldn't decide if his relentless teenage optimism in the face of all this chaos and murder was brave or stupid or maybe a little bit of both.

"I won't," I said.

He leaned across the seat and threw his arms around me in an intense, breathtakingly tight hug. Me, I've never been much of a hugger. I've been told a million times that I've got intimacy issues, and I suppose it's probably true. It's one of the few things my uptight shrink Lindsey actually got right. To be honest, I would have felt much more comfortable giving Cody a blow job.

Eventually, he let me go and got out. I scooted over into the driver's seat and watched him cross the street without looking, causing an old Mexican lady in a Corolla to swear at him in Spanish as she passed.

I should have felt relieved, but I couldn't shake this sense of nauseous dread. I'd spent the last nine days at Duncan's working very hard at not thinking about my own situation. Duncan was a don't ask, don't tell kinda guy and I didn't have any real answers anyway. I knew eventually I needed to come up with some kind of realistic long-term plan, but I was so worn down, so emotionally drained and numb and empty inside, that I really didn't believe in any kind of happily ever after. My plan to escape all this and start a new life abroad someplace warm and beautiful suddenly seemed just as childish and fantastical now as it did when an old friend suggested it the night before he died. More so, even.

But of all the brilliant plans I might have made, hanging around in front of a police station waiting to get noticed was at the bottom of the list. If the guys who were after me had been able to find me in WitSec, they clearly had deep and powerful law enforcement connections and would be able to find me the second I created even the smallest blip in the system. Better to keep moving, keep my head down and stay off the radar. Vic's kid was going to have to sink or swim on his own.

I was just about to drive away when Lovell's horny toad and his big Native American pal got out of a dusty Range Rover and walked up to the door of the police station.

8.

Back when I'd heard that familiar Croatian voice in Lindsey's office, it was horrible and terrifying but in a strange way it was exactly what I needed. Like everything came into sharp, clear focus. I could breathe again. I had been living this fake life, trying to be this fake person who'd never existed, and then in that instant, I became my real self again.

Driving away from Lindsey's, from that impossible voice and whatever kind of hell was taking place inside that office, I started running a checklist in my head. Car was gassed up, since I never allowed the tank to go below half full. Still had the shovel in my trunk. Gym bag on the passenger seat with a spare set of clothes. Nearly a grand in the slim fanny pack I wore all the time, even when I slept. The things in my apartment were irrelevant. Set dressing for a dull sitcom that had been canceled due to poor ratings. But I had other things, things that mattered. I hadn't told Lindsey about those things, because she would have said that I was being paranoid, not letting go of the past.

In a rundown, industrial neighborhood near the train tracks there was an abandoned gas station. The garage had been torn down and all that was left was the rusted pumps, some broken concrete and a lot of weedy dirt. Not enough of a structure left to entice bored local kids looking for someplace to practice their wannabe gang graffiti, drink beer and/or get pregnant. It was perfect for me.

I passed by twice to make sure I wasn't followed, then pulled in and popped the trunk for the shovel. The day was bright and the sun felt like a spotlight, but there was nobody around. A car passed without slowing, then a lumbering truck. I waited another minute, then walked back to a rusted car frame nearly buried in the weeds.

Gnats buzzed around my head and the smell of crushed green stalks under my sneakers was far too summery and innocent to fit the seriousness of my situation. When I reached the frame I took five steps from the front of the area that would have housed the engine and started digging.

The small military surplus footlocker I uncovered had been there for over a year. It was dirty, but otherwise none the worse for wear. No one saw me pull it up out of the hole I'd dug except for a scattering of frightened pill bugs.

Inside was a sturdy backpack, which I removed, leaving the footlocker behind. It contained cash, about four grand, spare clothes and running shoes, a Sig P232, a couple hundred rounds, and a pretty decent fake ID from New Hampshire that said my name was Jennifer Tate.

I put the backpack in the trunk and drove a few hours down the 95. After I crossed the state line, I pulled into a Denny's. I waited till a young couple got into their car and drove away before I got out, casing the lot. Plenty of cars but no humans. I took the backpack and my gym bag but left the shovel in the trunk. I hated to do it, but I knew I had to ditch the car, since it was registered to Lena Morrow, my now clearly compromised WitSec name.

I went into the restaurant and spent a good long minute evaluating the customers. I was looking for single men and spotted three that looked promising. Bachelor number one was a tall, gangly older man with a bald head and a tired hound-dog face sitting at the counter and staring at the remains of his Grand Slam. Bachelor number two was a handsome young Latino with longish hair who couldn't take his eyes off my tits. Bachelor number three was a sunburned redneck in a tractor cap with a gold cross around his neck.

The redneck was obviously religious, which meant horny and probably not getting any at home. Would be easy to tempt into sin, but also might go too far and turn out to be a serial killer. The Latino guy looked like he would follow my pussy anywhere, but got disqualified when an annoyed girlfriend returned from the bathroom and caught him staring at me. That left number one, who had seemed like the best bet from the beginning. He had the burned-out, weary body language of a man on a long, boring road trip and I figured he'd be thrilled to have company. I was right.

His name was Jim Falmworth and he owned a small company that manufactured a machine for stimulating injured muscles with electric pulses at varying strengths and speeds. He was traveling down the east coast, visiting the offices of chiropractors and physical therapists to try and sell them the new improved version of the machine. He liked anal sex, but his wife wouldn't do it. I would. I rode with Jim all the way to South Carolina.

9.

If I had a dime for every time I thought I ought to get gone but didn't, I'd be able to buy my own tropical island. Needless to say, I didn't drive away. I stayed, sweating and waiting in the driver's seat. I kept trying to tell myself the two men were there for some other reason that had nothing to do with Cody, but I knew in my heart that I'd been foolish to trust the authorities to save the day. I, of all people, should have known better.

Minutes later, my fears were confirmed when the two men came back out bookending a pale and frightened Cody. They bundled him into the back of the Rover so fast there was no time to think, to figure out what I ought to do. They pulled out, and for lack of a better idea, I followed them.

Not that I had a clue what I was going to do if I caught up with them. I just had it in my mind that I couldn't let them make Cody disappear. They were flying south on 95 and the traffic was light enough to make me paranoid about being spotted. The landscape was mostly dull, agricultural. We passed the Kikima Casino that Cody had mentioned, a squat, glittery building that had the used-up, shabby glamour of a hooker in the morning. I was starting to worry that they were planning on crossing the border when they suddenly slowed and turned into the driveway of one of several McMansions. Large but painfully tacky cookie-cutter homes that had been built right up against the highway despite the acres of empty land behind them. The one they entered was by far the largest of the group and also the most gleefully tasteless. An automatic iron gate decorated with snarling lions opened and shut behind the Rover. I had no choice but to keep driving.

When I felt I could pull a U-turn without attracting too much attention, I headed back for another pass. There was no place nearby that I could park without being completely obvious, so I just drove slowly past, trying to memorize every detail. Cody and the two men had already gone inside.

There was a fountain in the front yard featuring nude Greek nymphs that had been given a garish paint job. Peachy-orange skin, canary yellow hair and bright red nipples. Was this Lovell's house? There didn't seem to be a house number anywhere I could see, let alone anything as convenient as a name on a mailbox.

I didn't feel like I could turn around again so I just kept going.

It took some doing, but eventually I found my way back to Hank's martial arts school. I could see him through the window, demonstrating some kind of rolling, twisting maneuver that looked pretty similar to the one Cody had used to break the shooter's arm back in the diner. The students, a mixed-gender group between the ages of six and ten, then paired off and practiced rolling each other over and stretching each other's arms. Hank walked around the mat, correcting techniques here and there. He didn't notice me.

I killed the truck's engine and got out. It was already hot, but I felt a chilly coil of fear inside my belly that made me shiver as I walked over to the door of the school. The sign above it read "Richland MMA Academy" in peeling red letters. The same ugly logo on the t-shirt I'd slept in the night before. Beneath it, aggressive, spiky black lettering that looked designed in a high school study hall invited me to unleash my warrior spirit. I went inside.

There was a small reception area up front. A desk with no one sitting at it. A rack of shoes, above which a handwritten sign read, "NO shoes on the mat. NO EXCEPTIONS." To one side was a set of doors marked *Men's* and *Women's*. Between them was a glass case full of gloves, wraps and protective pads for sale, along with dusty copies of a cheaply bound autobiography by the eponymous Steve Richland, AAFC Champion. Above the case was a cluster of framed photos and trophy shelves, all dedicated to Richland and his wife, AWKA Muay Thai Champion Truly Richland.

The husband was handsome and square-jawed and apparently dead. In the center of all the photos, there was a large kitschy painting of Richland wearing fingerless gloves and a championship belt. A lurking Asian dragon floated behind him with a strange, oddly prurient look on its long, dog-like face and beneath him was his name and what had to be birth and death dates. The later date was five years ago.

The wife looked like she should be in the business. Bright red Miss America hair. Big fake tits. Collagen trout-pout. Tiny, surgically bobbed button nose. Her body was flawless, jacked and shredded, with an astounding bubble butt that looked like it could crack walnuts. She was in a g-string bikini in most of her photos, except the fight shots, in which she wore loose pink satin shorts and a sports bra. There was also a photo of the grieving widow standing graveside in a tacky and inappropriate dress that showed way too much plastic cleavage.

"Hi there," a female voice said behind me. "Are you one of the mothers?"

I turned to face the real live Truly Richland. There had clearly been a lot of Photoshop action in those pictures, but the body under her Richland MMA Academy tank top and tiny shorts was still amazing. She was my age or maybe a little older and had a brittle, anxious smile. Her voice was syrupy and Southern. Up close, her nose job was appalling. It made me glad I never got mine fixed.

"I'm..." I stumbled, suddenly unsure of what to say. I decided to see if I could dig up any dirt about Cody. "I'm looking for Cody Noon. Have you seen him?"

I was expecting something negative, related in some way to the supposed trouble that Cody was in, but the instant, napalm flare of jealousy in her eyes took me by surprise. She couldn't have conveyed the fact that she was fucking him more clearly if she'd shown me a video.

"How do you know Cody?" she asked, looking like she was about to slug me.

I backpedaled, trying to think fast. Behind me, two teenage boys tumbled through the door and plopped down on the bench beside the shoe rack, horsing around, snickering and texting one-handed while removing their sneakers.

"I'm his father's girlfriend," I said, wondering if she'd heard anything about the shootout at the diner, if Vic's body had been found yet. "His father was worried, said he might be in trouble. Have you heard anything?"

She nodded, visibly relieved for a moment before she was

able to construct a more appropriate worried teacher kind of look.

"I don't know," she said. "But I hear rumors. Of course, I strongly discourage my students from participating in unsanctioned matches of any kind, but you know, boys will be boys."

At that point the phone on the desk rang.

"Will you excuse me?" Truly asked.

I nodded, and she turned to pick up the phone.

While she went into a detailed explanation of the membership fees, one of the two barefoot teenage boys on the bench spoke up.

"He's fucked."

I turned to the kids on the bench. The one who'd spoken looked a little older than his friend. He was Latino or maybe Native American with cornrowed hair and bad skin. His friend was a sunburned towhead with a goofy swooped-over-to-one-side hairstyle and submissive, beta-dog body language.

"Excuse me?" I took a step closer to them.

"Cody," the older kid said. "He's fucked."

"Why do you say that?" I asked.

"Come on, man," the towhead said out of the corner of his mouth, eyeing me like I might bite. "She could be a cop."

"Yeah, right," the older kid replied with a snort of lofty teenage derision. "She ain't no cop."

"How do you know?"

"Cause I know, *puto*." He punched the towhead in the arm. "You ain't," he said to me. "Right?"

"Right," I replied. "I'm just a friend."

The older kid stood.

"Okay, follow me," he said. "But take your shoes off."

I took my shoes off, put them on the rack and followed the two kids into a small weight room off to one side of the large blue mats that took up the majority of the long open space. Hank was still busy showing little kids how to break each other's bones. There was a large clock on the back wall that read 9:45.

"What time does that class end?" I asked.

"Ten," the older kid said. "Why?"

"I need to talk to Hank. It's important."

The kid nodded and then led me over to a row of lockers on the far side of the weight room. I noticed a black vinyl man-shaped dummy leaning drunkenly against the wall by the weight rack. Someone had slipped a pair of pink lace panties over its stiff cylindrical legs. Its smooth blank face seemed to be watching us.

"So…Mr. Lovell, he sets up these fights down in San Luis, on the other side of the border. Guys who fight down there, like Cody, well, Mr. Lovell has them bring stuff home with them. Bodybuilding supplements that you can't get in the States."

"Supplements?" I said. "You mean like steroids?"

"I don't mean vitamins," he said.

The towheaded kid was looking increasingly uncomfortable about the topic of conversation. He slowly drifted away and started hitting the heavy bag with his bare knuckles.

"Does Cody use steroids?" I asked, not sure why I even cared, but hoping the answer would be no.

The kid shook his head.

"Nah," he said. "He's all obsessed on the AAFC. They test."

"Okay, so then what kind of trouble is he in?" I asked. "What does this have to do with steroids?"

"Well, they pack the shit into jars of protein powder and you supposed to leave the jars in your locker after you get across the border. Mr. Lovell sends his guys to pick 'em up the next morning and leaves an envelope of cash. Only when they went to pick up Cody's shipment, it was light."

"I thought you said he doesn't use steroids," I said, frowning and looking over at the battered wall of lockers.

"He don't," the kid said, rolling his eyes like I was the dumbest bitch he'd ever met. "But he uses money."

Jesus. The motorcycle. The expensive clothes. The money he owed. But why steal from Lovell to pay him back? Unless Cody was never planning on paying Lovell back at all. Maybe he assumed he would be safe once he got on TV. No way to find out now. Maybe not ever, if Lovell decided it would be best just to bury Cody out in the desert. Maybe he already had and none of this mattered.

I looked up at the clock. It was ten. The kids' class had wrapped and Hank was standing alone at the corner of the mat, squinting and lost in thought.

I thanked the cornrowed kid for the info and walked over to Hank. When he heard my bare footsteps on the mat, he looked up and flashed that broad, boyish grin. He didn't seem even remotely surprised to see me.

"We need to talk," I said.

The smile faltered slightly.

"Well, okay," he said.

"Not here." I looked around. Students in their teens and early twenties were crowding in while harried parents corralled the younger kids and herded them out the front door. "Somewhere private."

"All right," he said, taking my arm and leading me into a small office behind the weight room. "But you'd better make it quick. I got another class coming in."

This office was also decorated with framed photos and trophies, but these celebrated the illustrious fight career of one Hank "The Hammer" Hammond. I was anxious and distracted but I couldn't help noticing that the most recent item was dated 2002.

"Lovell's got Cody," I said as soon as the door was shut behind us.

"God…" he started, but swallowed the curse before it was out. "…bless America." He passed his hand over his eyes. "What happened?"

I explained everything I'd seen and added what the cornrowed kid had told me.

"Lovell ain't gonna kill him," Hank said. "Not yet anyway."

"What makes you so sure?" I asked.

"Because he wants his money's worth. If Cody's dead he can't fight, and if he can't fight, he can't throw it and make back what Lovell lost on him last week."

I nodded, tried to focus, to come up with some brilliant plan that would save Cody's life, but my eye kept on going back to a large photo of a not exactly handsome, but younger, less battered Hank with his gloved fists up, wearing tiny black shorts and nothing else. I was all out of brilliant.

"So what do we do?" I asked.

"Well," he said, then paused, frowning. "What did you say your name was again?"

I looked into his pale eyes to see if he was joking. He wasn't. I was starting to get the feeling that maybe he'd been hit in the head one too many times.

"Angel," I said.

"Well, Angel, here's how I figure it. We got until at least nine PM so there's no point getting all bent out of shape right now. I'm on the card tonight too, so after I'm done here for the day, you and I'll just head down to San Luis like everything was normal. You'll need to do the driving, of course, since I ain't allowed no more on account of my migraines."

"I don't have a real driver's license," I said. "In fact, I don't have any legit ID at all, so there's no way I can go across the border."

Hank smiled and shook his huge head.

"Ain't we a pair?" he said. "Why'd they take yours away?"

"It's a long story," I said.

"Well then you can tell it on the way to San Luis," he said.

"I just told you I can't do that," I said.

"Sure you can," Hank said. "I know all the border guards and they pretty much don't give a damn about anyone American going out. Especially pretty Americans like you. Coming back'll be a different story, but we can cross that bridge when we get there."

"I just can't take that chance," I said. I knew how serious things had become at border crossings what with the terrorist hysteria all over the world. That was the reason I had been so dead set on scoring a new passport, the whole reason I'd been with Duncan in the first place. I had been so damn close too, before all this.

"Look," Hank said. "We'll talk more about this after I'm

done teaching. In the meanwhile, you're welcome to hang out here. You can work out, use the weights or hit the bags. If you like, you can even take one of my classes. The first one's free."

"I've never…" I looked back up at the wall of photos, eye falling on a shot of Hank standing in the ring with his face masked in blood, a Japanese ref raising his hand. "I mean, I've done some kickboxing, just for fitness. Never anything like this."

"This next one coming up is probably more advanced than you'd want for starters," he said. "But the after-lunch class is for beginners. All you gotta do is sign a waiver up front agreeing it ain't my fault if you drop dead."

I grinned.

"If I die, you gotta promise to do whatever needs to be done to save Cody," I said.

"You bet," Hank said. "That boy's like my own. I ain't gonna let him down."

10.

I spent the next hour at Richland's MMA Academy skipping rope and lifting weights. Pushing myself to the edge of my endurance and trying not to think about Cody. There was nothing I could do about the situation. Either Hank was right and Lovell wouldn't hurt Cody until after the fight, or he was wrong and it was already too late.

But what I could do was try to figure out a way to get my hands on the passport Duncan had promised me.

I met Duncan Schenck through a chain of unwashed, wild-eyed cranks, survivalists, and other assorted non-citizens living off the grid at varying levels of arrested sexual development and personal hygiene. Most were either genuinely bug-fuck crazy or utterly full of shit, perpetual teenagers living out their own personal late-'80s post-apocalyptic movie fantasies. I'm sure there are a million smarter, faster, better ways to go about securing a fake passport, but I'm willing to bet most of them would involve way more money than I could scrape together blowing truckers for a year.

The guy who tipped me to Duncan was fat and acerbic with a surprisingly handsome face behind his smudgy coke-bottle glasses. He wouldn't tell me his own name, but he did allow that maybe this guy Schenck could help me. It was his understanding that this guy Schenck had connections, but that he would only help women. Pretty women. Sounded like my kinda guy.

I showed up near closing time at Duncan's Diner in the one dress I still owned. I had lipstick on for the first time in over a week. I sat at the counter and drank coffee and flirted with him through the pass and when it was midnight, he asked me if I had anywhere to go and I batted my lashes and tearfully admitted that I didn't, that I was broke and alone and just drinking coffee because I didn't have enough money for food. He made me a steak and told me that his little trailer out back didn't look like much, but it was real cozy.

After I'd paid for my steak, we lay together in his narrow bed and I started to tell the story I'd concocted about an abusive boyfriend who was a cop and how I needed to disappear, to leave the States. Duncan cut me off and told me he didn't need to know any of the gory details. That if I wanted to disappear, that was all he needed to hear. That he would help me, no questions asked. Of course, he understood that I didn't have the kind of money it would take to secure a whole new identity, including a flawless passport complete with phony travel history. But I shouldn't worry my pretty little head about that, because even though something like that normally cost nearly ten thousand dollars, Uncle Duncan had connections. Uncle Duncan would take care of everything, just so long as I continued to take care of him. He said a woman like me didn't need money anyway, but that he would be happy to give me a job waiting tables, off the books of course, so I could have a little extra to buy some pretty clothes while I was waiting on the fake passport. I didn't tell him about the three grand or so I still had tucked into my money belt.

He made arrangements for a cute young Latino guy to come over and take my photo, but I never met anyone else involved in the process. Duncan insisted that his so-called connections were bad, dangerous men and he didn't want me anywhere near them. For my own safety, of course. He certainly did have a fairly constant stream of shifty-eyed and disreputable-looking visitors on any given day. But once he started to trust me and took me down into the bunker under his trailer to show off his "babies," I realized those visitors had nothing to do with fake passports.

I mentioned earlier that Duncan was a firearms enthusiast but what I didn't mention is that he was particularly enthusiastic about a certain class of firearm, the private ownership of which is heavily frowned upon by the state of Arizona. I also didn't mention that he shared his enthusiasm with fellow collectors from all over the country for an obscene amount of under-the-table income.

The night before Vic showed up and everything went to hell in a handbasket, I had asked Duncan, in the most girly, helpless and non-threatening way, of course, if he thought maybe my passport might be ready soon. He told me he just needed to pay the second half of what he owed on it and then he figured it would be good to go in another day or two. That's exactly what he'd been saying for nearly two weeks. I was starting to wonder if maybe he was playing me, but I was in no position to do anything but wait. Then the whole shootout thing happened and it was out of my hands.

But I couldn't let it end there. There had to be a way to get that passport and as I skipped, I started to put together the bones of a possible plan. No way to know if it would work but to try it and find out, but it would have to wait until Hank's classes were over. Nothing to do now but sweat and wait.

11.

I signed up for Hank's class with Truly, officially accepting all liability for anything from a stubbed toe to a broken neck. I figured I could use a few more tips on how to hurt people.

The class was mostly teens, with a few men in their early twenties. I was easily the oldest person in the class. There were only two other females. One was a piece of trashy blond jailbait with a tribal tramp stamp and a chip on her shoulder. The other was a shy Native American baby butch. Unlike me, they both knew what they were in for.

Now I'm in pretty good shape. I'd even say great shape. I work out compulsively and I'm pretty proud of my stamina but I'll tell you what, I got served up a double scoop of humility in the first ten minutes of Hank's "beginner" class.

It started off with running around in a circle. Easy enough. Then several variations on running: sideways, lunging, crawling and a kind of crouching duckwalk. After that, shadowboxing combos, falling flat on our bellies and bouncing back up again, and then bridges, reaching back over our heads as we pushed our pelvises toward the ceiling.

By the time we started a particularly sadistic exercise that involved sitting with our backs against the wall and then "climbing" to a standing position using only our shoulder muscles, I was close to throwing up. The actual grappling hadn't even started yet and I was ready to give up. I didn't. I stuck with it. I didn't want Hank to think I was a wimp.

When the warm-ups ended, I got paired up with the angry jailbait. She said her name was Lynette and that she was from Ohio originally but had moved to Yuma to live with her grandmother when her parents divorced. Said she was saving up to move to Los Angeles when she turned eighteen. There was no doubt in my mind that she would end up in the business.

We started off practicing something called "breaking the closed guard." It seemed real simple when Hank demonstrated but somehow it got all backwards when I tried it.

"Do you know Cody Noon?" I asked Lynette on a hunch, kneeling between her legs like we were about to do a strap-on scene.

"Yeah," she said, drawing the word out into two long syllables as she wrapped her legs around my waist. "He was, like, the first guy in class that I hooked up with." She leaned in close and dropped her voice to a conspiratorial whisper. "And oh my God, he's got the biggest dick I've ever seen in real life."

I smiled and shook my head, not even remotely surprised by this revelation. Was Cody sleeping with every straight female in Yuma? That didn't surprise me either. I gripped the waist of Lynette's shorts, scooted my knee up underneath her ass and felt around inside her thighs with the points of my elbows.

"I think you gotta put your other knee up first," Lynette said.

Then, suddenly Hank was there beside us.

"Go on," he said. "Try it again."

I did like he told me, but it still didn't feel right. He motioned for Lynette to get up and then knelt down beside me on the mat.

"Come on now," he said, lying back on the mat with his legs open and holding his hands out to me. "Get into my guard."

I did as he requested and he wrapped his legs around my waist, pulling me close in a kind of weird reverse missionary position. I was intensely aware of his crotch pressing against my belly. He smelled good. I was pretty sure that I didn't.

"Isn't this supposed to be the other way around?" I joked to cover my embarrassment.

"No," he said, face solemn and serious. "This is right."

So much for my rapier wit.

"Now you need to make sure you're really hitting that pressure point inside and just above the knee." He slid his hand casually down my inner thigh. "Right here."

I shivered, then stifled a girly yelp as he pressed his thumb into the soft spot inside my knee, sending a sharp shooting pain up the inside of my leg.

"Got it?" he asked.

I nodded. My face felt hot. Being so close to him was making me stupid and I needed three more tries before I was able to make the damn move work, but he stayed cool and stuck with me until I got it right.

It was much easier with Lynette, but I found I couldn't stop watching Hank out of the corner of my eye. I kinda hoped maybe he was watching me too. If he was, I never caught him.

He really was a gifted teacher. Patient but uncompromising, attentive and encouraging to each individual student and very, very serious about grappling. When he was teaching, he was completely focused. No sign of that absent-minded forgetfulness. I could see why Cody idolized him.

By the time the hour was up, I felt ready for the retirement home. I had taken an accidental elbow from Lynette that didn't quite black my eye but gave me a nice bruise just below the eyebrow. Every joint in my body hurt, especially my shoulders. All my core muscles ached like I was wearing a hot iron corset.

"Great job, Angel," Hank said. "You're a real quick study."

"I don't feel very quick at the moment," I said.

"You did better than most your first time out," he said. "You got a lot of natural ability. You're very strong for your size and your flexibility is excellent, especially in the hips."

"You don't know the half of it," I said.

That time, he got it. He blushed.

"Well…" he began but trailed off.

I know it's petty, but I felt much better.

I showered in the women's room, my second shower of the day. I was happy to discover they had both shampoo and conditioner. Out and dry, I changed into my last set of clean clothes. Fixing my damp hair and checking myself out in the mirror, I inventoried my assets with a critical eye. I was a little heavier than I might have liked, but the extra weight was well distributed, filling out my tits and making my face look smoother and more youthful than it did when I was thinner. And while I'd given up dieting, I had focused instead on getting stronger and building endurance. As a result I'd gotten much thicker than I used to be. Fatter maybe, but tougher. I still looked pretty good.

I realized that even though it was probably a Very Bad Idea, I was planning to jump Hank's bones the first chance I got.

Then I thought about Vic and Cody and what I was doing here in the first place and felt a swift chill of guilt. I needed to quit letting my pussy drive and stay focused on getting Cody out of the trouble he was in. Everything else needed to take a back seat.

But I pulled my tank top down to show a little more cleavage. Because hey, it didn't hurt to look good along the way.

12.

Hank was waiting by the front desk. He had showered again, too, and changed into jeans and a sleeveless t-shirt. He noticed the extra cleavage right away and made a big show of not looking down.

"I have an idea," I told him. "I'll fill you in on the way."

In his truck and heading north, I told him all about Duncan and the passport. I told him about a guy named Lenny, no last name that I knew of, who was a member of what Duncan referred to as the F.A.A.A. or Full Auto Association of America. He was the only one of Duncan's friends whose home I'd actually visited.

"Weirdest dinner party I've ever been to," I told Hank. "Lenny's spooky, silent teenage wife serving our food like some kind of slave. She didn't eat anything because, according to Lenny, she was too fat. Said he'd been forced to put her on a diet. She couldn't have weighed more than 115 pounds. He's the same height and closer to 250."

"Sounds like a real gem," Hank said. "Why do we want to pay this guy a visit again?"

"Because," I said. "He's the only person I can think of who might know who's got my passport."

"How much you reckon Duncan still owes on that passport anyway?" he asked.

I shrugged.

"Duncan said it'd normally cost ten grand, but he might

have been exaggerating just to make me more grateful. I've got no idea how much he's already paid, if anything. In fact, I wouldn't put it past him to have made the whole thing up just to get into my pants."

"I could see as how that might be the case," Hank said. "Beautiful woman like you must get all kinds of B.S. from men pretty much every day of the week."

"Yeah, well..." I smiled. "Only one way to find out."

We pulled up to the first security gate on Lenny's private road. I leaned out the driver's-side window so that the camera could see my cleavage as well as my face.

"State your business," a staticky voice demanded though a small plastic speaker.

"Lenny," I said. "It's Julie. Isn't it awful about Duncan? Listen I really need to talk to you."

A buzzer sounded and the automatic gate swung slowly open.

"Julie?" Hank said, frowning. "Where did I get Angel? I was sure I had that right."

"My name really is Angel," I said. I didn't bother to tell him that name was made up too, even though it seemed more real to me than the one I was born with. "I just don't want Lenny to know my real name."

"Oh yeah, right," he said with all the solemn intensity of a kid who's just been made to pinkie-swear. "Okay, you can count on me. I won't say nothing."

"Thanks," I said. "Just hang back and let me do the talking."

We had to zigzag through two more heavy steel gates before we finally arrived at Lenny's cheerless concrete-block bunker. Lenny himself stood in the open doorway to greet us, dressed in jaunty hibiscus-print swimming trunks and a shoulder holster. His corpulent body was covered in thick white hair, like a small, upright polar bear. He looked way too oily to have been swimming and I didn't remember him having a pool anyway

"Who's he?" he asked with a suspicious squint and a tilt of his several chins in Hank's direction.

"Just a friend," I said. "I've been afraid to be alone since—"

"You'd better come inside," Lenny said. He lifted a tiny pair of binoculars to his eyes and looked down the road. "It ain't safe out here."

On the inside, Lenny's fortress was decorated with paintings that looked like they belonged on the side of someone's party van from the early '80s. Wolves and flames and large-breasted women with swords. The furniture in the big main room was a sorry collection of mismatched junk that I was afraid to sit on in shorts. The carpet was stained and unspeakable. There was a major infestation of beer cans, piled up in drifts at the corners of the room. Lenny noticed me looking at the cans and shouted:

"Layla, you lazy bitch, get your fat ass in here!"

Layla, the homely little teen bride, slunk into the room in pink flannel PJ bottoms, a nearly see-through tank top and bunny slippers. It was about 5 PM.

"I thought I told you to clean up this mess," Lenny said.

He picked up a can and threw it at her. The can bounced off her hip and rolled away but she didn't react. She just bent down and started picking the cans up.

"All right then," he said to me, ignoring Hank. "Step into my office."

Hank and I followed him down a narrow hallway and into his office. Not that he actually did any kind of work that I was aware of. From what I understood, Lenny lived off some kind of settlement and spent the majority of his time trolling liberal bloggers and sending out anonymous death threats to politicians who supported gun control legislation or "sodomy and pedophilia," meaning gay rights.

The cheesy art on his office walls featured more big-breasted women in less clothing. Most of them had guns. There was no other furniture besides the desk and office chair. Lenny parked one beefy ass cheek on the edge of the desk and gave me a leisurely once over.

"So what did you want to talk about?" he asked.

I took a few seconds to collect my wits, to figure the best approach. It was a safe bet that he had, in addition to the ostentatious .44 AutoMag in his sweaty armpit, at least three or four other guns within easy reach anywhere in the office. Brute force probably wasn't gonna work. I had to play it right or I wasn't gonna get another chance.

"Have you heard anything about the guys who shot Duncan?" I asked.

Lenny shook his head.

"Just some dumbass wetbacks," he said. "Trying to rob the place, I guess. I heard they found this guy dead in his car out on Indian Rock Road. Turns out he's a big time porn star from Los Angeles. They're still trying to figure out how he fits into the picture." He narrowed his eyes. "You wouldn't know anything about that, huh?"

I shook my head, heart cold. Had he made me as Angel Dare? Searched online and uncovered the whole ugly nightmare I'd been through? Was he thinking he could blackmail me somehow?

"You know the cops are looking for you, Julie," he said.

"That's what I was afraid of," I replied, fighting to keep my voice slow and calm. "That's why I need to get that passport ASAP. You don't happen to know the guy who Duncan hired to make it for me, do you?"

"Yeah," he said. "But you don't want anything to do with a dangerous guy like that."

"I don't really have a choice, do I?"

"Well, sure you do," Lenny said. "See, I might be willing to intervene on your behalf, given the proper motivation. Duncan was like a brother to me and he spoke very highly of you. Very highly."

I could see where this was going long before Lenny leaned in and said, "He told me you can just about suck a man's heart out though the tip of his cock."

I sighed, already resigned to what I was going to have to do to get that passport, but since Hank was standing behind and to the left of me, I didn't see him tensing up like an angry cobra. All I saw was a burst of sudden movement as he shot in and knocked Lenny's lecherous grin right off his face.

Lenny dropped liked he'd been shot, crumpling sideways and bouncing his head off the corner of the desk on the way down. He was out before he could even think of going for his gun.

The second he was down, I reached in and snatched the heavy AutoMag from his armpit. His legs were twitching like a dreaming dog and he was making a funny kind of loose-lipped snoring sound.

"Hank," I said. "He could have killed you."

"Well, I wasn't about to stand here and let him talk to you like that." Hank knelt down beside me, hauled the lolling Lenny up by the holster strap and shook him. "Ain't got no more dirty talk now, do ya?"

Lenny made some wet, non-verbal noises like a passed-out drunk, eyelids fluttering and head rolling from side to side. Hank gripped Lenny's hand, twisting it around and folding it up towards the wrist. One of Lenny's mumbled half-words sharpened into a yelp of pain. Lenny's eyes went wide but still not entirely aware.

"You want to talk about something," Hank said. "How about telling the lady where she can get her passport?"

"Fuck!" Lenny said and was about to say it again, when Hank twisted his wrist up higher, eliciting another screech.

"I swear," Hank said, "If I hear one more word out of your filthy mouth that ain't an address, I'm gonna start breaking fingers."

I stepped back and drew a bead on Lenny's sweating forehead with the AutoMag.

"You better do what the man says," I told him.

"All right, all right," Lenny said, suddenly sharp again. "Jesus. The guy's name is Earl Wyman. Lives just off the old golf course at Sierra Sands. 4515 East Nine Iron Drive."

"That's more like it," Hank said.

I set the AutoMag on Lenny's desk, yanked an extension cord from the wall and used it to hogtie him. He wasn't even remotely flexible and I struggled to get his hands close together behind his hairy back. The thin cord dug deep into his wrists, his fingers going cold and blue before I was even finished tying his ankles.

"I'm gonna find you," Lenny was saying, twisting up on his side with flecks of spit flying from his lips. "See if I don't, you fucking bitch!"

Hank hauled back and kicked him hard in the chest, just below the right pectoral muscle. Lenny went white, let out a breathless grunt and would have curled up like a fetus if he hadn't been tied up.

"What'd I tell you about that kind of talk?" Hank asked. "Now unless you want me to kick your liver into the next county, you'd best mind your manners."

He cocked his leg back like he was about to make good on the threat and Lenny cringed and squealed, squeezing his eyes closed.

"Oh God, Jesus, don't," he wheezed. "Please God."

We left Lenny begging and dry heaving in his office. On the way out I spotted mousy Layla standing in the living room with a plastic bag full of beer cans. Lenny was calling out to her to let him loose. She looked at me sideways through her hair for a moment, but made no move to help Lenny. She just bent down and continued picking up the beer cans.

13.

The Sierra Sands golf course seemed abandoned, sad and neglected, its once improbably lush greens being swiftly reclaimed by the desert around it. There were a few large, upscale homes in the area, but more than half were either for sale or in foreclosure. Nine Iron Drive was a long swath of stillborn potential, plot after empty plot waiting for homes that would never be built. Down near the dead end of the street stood a single orphan house.

The house looked as if it had been plucked, Dorothy-like, from some nice retirement community and dropped here by a fickle tornado. It had a generic faux-Spanish style with a terracotta tile roof, peach stucco walls and a cute little succulent garden out front. There was a kitschy wooden sign shaped like a saguaro cactus that read CARR & WYMAN. Not exactly what you'd expect from a dangerous criminal.

I sat for a minute in Hank's truck, taking stock of the situation. I reached into my go-bag, checked the Sig over and then handed it to Hank.

"I really don't have any idea what to expect," I said, taking the tiny Warthog for myself and wishing I had kept Lenny's AutoMag. "Obviously we'd prefer to settle this without violence, but that didn't work so well with Lenny so I figure it's better to be prepared."

As we walked up the crushed gravel path to the front

door, I took a moment to consider how to explain to Hank that if the best way to settle this turned out to be a blow job, then he'd better be ready to back off and let me do it.

The man who opened the door was in his mid-to-late sixties, short and very tan with large, clunky black glasses dominating his small, triangular face. He had a jaunty red bandana tied around his neck, a large gold pinky ring and a glossy, chestnut toupee.

"Can I help you?" he asked, blinking owlishly through his thick glasses.

"I'm..." I paused, trying to figure out what to say. "I'm a friend of Duncan's."

"Ah," he replied. "I thought I recognized you. You'd better come inside."

We did. There were no armed guards. No attack dogs. No visible security of any kind. Just a pleasant, comfortable living room with a fat, sleeping cat perched on the back of the sofa. The walls were covered with intense, almost photo-realistic paintings of dusty, weathered cowboys. When I looked closer, I saw the signature. Wyman.

"Normally," the man said, "I don't deal directly with the clients. That was part of the agreement. However, under the circumstances... It's awful, isn't it?"

"Awful," I agreed. "These your paintings?"

"Why, yes, they are," he said with a pleased flash of teeth too perfect to be natural. "That's my real work. I just do this other thing... Well you see, my..."

He looked up at a photo on the mantel of two smiling young men in cowboy hats, circa 1975. There were no other family photos.

"My...my wife passed away recently," he said. "There were a lot of bills."

"I'm so sorry," I said.

I'd realized by then that a blow job wasn't gonna be an option. Not from me, anyway. I wanted to tell Wyman he didn't need to lie to me about the gender of his dead partner, but before I could come up with a tactful way to say it, he changed the subject.

"Your friend there has quite a face," he said. "You can see stories in that face. I'd love to paint him." He turned to Hank. "Any chance I might convince you to sit for me some time?"

"Paint me?" Hank smiled. "With all due respect, sir, I think you need some new glasses."

"I don't paint pretty faces," Wyman said. "I paint real faces. A pretty face is boring, meaningless, like a toothpaste ad. Trust me, I ought to know. I worked in advertising for thirty-five years and when I retired I swore I'd never paint a pretty face again."

"Well," Hank said. "I ain't pretty, that's for sure."

"Come on into the studio," Wyman said. "Let's get that other business taken care of."

We followed Wyman down a hallway and into his studio. I guess I was expecting something more old school. Oil paints and canvases and brushes and easels and all that. Of course those things were there too, but the majority of the large room was dominated with several top-of-the-line computers, a bank of huge monitors and an enormous laser printer. Several pro-grade cameras, both digital and analog. A tilted Wacom Cintiq displayed a half-completed drawing of a granite-faced Mexican man with a pistol. All these things were interesting and intriguing, but my eye went instantly to a semi-transparent glassine envelope sitting on the desk. Inside the envelope was a distinct navy rectangle that had to be a passport. My passport.

"So," I said as casually as I could. "What do I owe you?"

Wyman frowned.

"Nothing," he said, handing me the envelope. "Duncan paid in full up front. It's been ready and waiting for him to pick up for over a week."

I laughed before I could help myself. Fucking Duncan. That figured.

"However, if you're feeling generous and could spare a few minutes," Wyman said. "I'd love to take a few quick photos of your not-so-pretty friend."

I shrugged.

"Hank?"

"I don't have to take my clothes off or nothing?"

"Certainly not," Wyman replied.

"Then I don't see why not," Hank said.

While Wyman shot close-up photos of Hank's face displaying a variety of emotions, I looked over my passport. I was surprised to find a matching driver's license tucked in between the pages. Both it and the passport were works of art. Soft, slightly worn around the edges but not overly so, like they'd been in my purse forever. The passport was dated a little less than three years ago, and in that time I'd apparently had five trips outside the States. The UK, Costa Rica, the Bahamas and twice to Mexico. My new name was Janet Miller. I worried briefly about Hank being able to remember a new name, but figured Angel sounded enough like a pet name that it wouldn't really raise eyebrows.

"Okay," Wyman said to Hank. "Now how about regret."

"Regret?" Hank asked.

"Just think about something you wish you hadn't done," Wyman said. The flash went off. "Perfect! That's fantastic!"

I turned back to Hank and saw the expression that had made Wyman so happy. I wondered what Hank was thinking about.

"Great," Wyman said. "Could I just get a few quick shots of your hands?"

Hank held out his hands, crushed knuckles up. He looked over Wyman's shoulder at me. The camera flashed.

"Now fists please," Wyman said.

Hank obliged.

"Those fists tell as many stories as your face," Wyman said, holding up the camera and checking over the shots on the small digital screen. "Beautiful. Thank you so much for taking the time to indulge an old fart and his silly hobby."

"No problem," Hank said.

"You picked yourself a good man," Wyman said to me. "A real man. You know Hollywood is full of beautiful empty men, but real men are an endangered species."

I smiled.

"Thanks for this," I said, holding up the passport.

"I suppose my short-lived criminal career is over now," Wyman said with a rueful smile. "Or maybe I'll try my hand at counterfeiting. I do a mean Ben Franklin."

He showed us to the door.

14.

The drive to Mexico was sweltering inside Hank's un-air-conditioned truck. Despite my recent shower, I was already feeling grimy and unlovely, drenched in sweat with desert dust in my hair. Hank was sweating, too, in the passenger seat, but it looked sexy on him. He was so ugly it went beyond ugly and became hot somehow. I just seemed to be getting more and more into him, the more time we spent together. It was this huge illogical, purely physical thing that I needed like a fucking hole in my head with everything else going on, but I just couldn't seem to stop myself from staring at him. It was a real struggle to keep my eyes on the road.

"Where are you from originally, Hank?" I asked, just to say something other than *I'll die if you don't fuck me right now*.

"Reidsville, North Carolina," he replied. "Left when I was seventeen and ain't never been back. How about you?"

"I grew up in Chicago," I said. "Then moved to Los Angeles and never went back."

"Do you miss it?" he asked. "Chicago I mean."

"I miss the city," I said. "But not my family."

"I hear that," he said. "I sure don't miss all my good-for-nothing cousins and uncles and in-laws back in Reidsville. My momma died from cancer just three months after she lost her job at the Lucky Strike factory. With her gone, there weren't no reason to stick around."

After we'd chewed up some more highway, I said, "Tell me about Lovell."

"Lovell," Hank said, shaking his head. "Well, he's half Indian, or claims to be. To be honest, you just never know what's true or what ain't with Vernon Lovell. I've been working for him about four years. He was pretty much the only person who would give me the time of day after…well…when I got out."

"Got out?" I frowned. "From prison?"

Hank nodded and looked away out the passenger window, then pulled a pill bottle from his hip pocket and dry swallowed a pair.

"What for?" I asked.

"Assault," he said without meeting my gaze. "It was stupid, just lost my temper and then three years of my life were gone. But truth is, I deserved a lot worse for what I done." He looked up at me, suddenly standoffish. "Reckon you don't want nothing to do with me now."

"Assault," I repeated, then laughed and shook my head. "That's nothing. I would have gone down for multiple murder if I hadn't agreed to testify against a bunch of scumbags who were importing underage Eastern Bloc girls for sex. I'm a cold-blooded killer, Hank. A 'vigilante.' I'm hardly in a position to judge other people's sins."

Hank's eyes went wide.

"Vigilante?" he repeated.

"Yeah," I said. That's what the headlines had called me. *Pornstar Vigilante. Dirty Harriet. Lady Killer.*

"I knew you was tough from the minute I laid eyes on you, but murder?" He shook his head. "That's really something. Whoever they were, I'll bet those guys deserved it."

"More than anyone I've ever met," I said.

We drove in silence for a sweltering minute. Then: "Wanna tell me about it?"

I looked over at Hank, then shook my head. That was a can of worms that didn't need opening.

"Some other time," I said. "Right now, I want to hear more about Lovell."

"Right," he said. "Well, when I first got out, I got myself into a fight with one of Lovell's boys. The kid wouldn't back down, kept on pushing me." He looked away. "Ended up putting him in the hospital. Lovell said he didn't see any reason to involve my parole officer in the matter, provided I was willing to go to work for him."

"So that's how you started teaching at Richland's?"

"Well, yeah. Lovell made Truly hire me on at the school so I had a legit-type job to keep my P.O. happy, but that's not the real work I do for Lovell."

I didn't say anything. I just drove until he was ready to continue.

"It's collection, mostly," Hank said with a shrug. "Anyone owes Lovell from the fights, I have a talk with 'em, make sure they pay up." He wiped the palms of his hands on his jeans like they were dirty. "I hate doing it, but if I don't, Lovell'd have me back inside before I knew what hit me. Lovell's got the local law deep in his pocket. It's like one of them catch-22s, because the more I do for him, the more he's got to hold over my head."

He was looking at me out of the corner of his eye, gauging my reaction. I drove without comment for a good minute before I spoke.

"Look, there are no good guys here," I said. "You do what you have to."

He nodded. That was the last of the conversation until we hit the border.

Crossing the border turned out to be no trouble at all. The new passport worked like a charm. Ten minutes later, we were in Mexico and on our way to Cody's fight.

15.

We had been driving through dusty Mexican nothing for so long, I would have gotten white-line fever if there had been any lines on the rutted dirt road. When we passed a dead car, it seemed way more exciting than it should have. A sad cluster of cement-block houses seemed like a bustling town. After the sun went down, I started to see pairs of bright, reflective eyes watching from the scrub brush on the sides of the road.

Then finally lights in the distance. Strobes in gaudy headache colors and way too much neon, like an impossible fever dream after the sensory deprivation of the dark desert. Our destination turned out to be this weird lost fragment of Vegas imprisoned behind barbed wire. A maximum security Señor Frog's.

A razorwire fence ran all the way around the place with a sliding gate standing open. The front of the long, narrow building was all molded to look like rock, with fake plastic orchids sticking out at random intervals and several small waterfalls spilling into scummy plastic basins full of greenish American pennies. A big throbbing red sign read CLUB OASIS and flickering neon women shifted their glowing hips robotically from side to side.

"Is this a strip club?" I asked, frowning at the bored-looking guy with body armor and an AK47 who waved us into the fenced parking area.

"It's an anything-you-can-afford club," Hank replied. "But the real action's in the back. Come on."

A red-vested pit crew of seven took over Hank's rickety truck the second we got out. Hank generously tipped everyone in sight, including the guy with the AK47, and then offered me his arm and escorted me to the main door.

The door was also made to look like stone, but felt like Styrofoam over sheet metal. More conspicuously armed guys greeted us inside when we entered, frisking me for a good three minutes before waving us through a red velvet curtain.

On the other side of the curtain was a short, obsequious man with no chin, a tight tuxedo and near perfect English. He fawned over Hank, calling him "Señor Hammer" and then leaning in to say that he had ten bucks on Hank's fight.

I ignored them both and checked out the club. They had pretty much given up the whole oasis theme by the time they'd gotten around to the interior design and had gone with a cheap black and gold faux deco look that was dated before I got into the business. Lots of dusty gold mirrors with black stripes.

There was a decent-sized main stage with a long catwalk to the left and four smaller go-go stations with poles on the right. There was no one on the stage at the moment, but all four smaller stations were in use and another six women worked the floor, trawling for lap dances or who knew what else.

The girls were surprisingly high-end. A lot of painfully obvious surgery and some pretty hard faces under the warpaint, but for the most part they were under thirty and better looking than some girls I'd worked with in L.A. The girls on the poles were full nude while the ones working the floor wore breathtakingly tacky stripper gowns in cheap, stretchy fabrics. I watched as one of the floor girls sat down beside a mustachioed guy who looked like an extra from a *narcotrafficante* movie, unzipped his jeans and started giving him a casual handjob. She wasn't making any attempt to hide what she was doing. That's when I noticed that every table had its own complimentary gold tissue box.

The girls all mad-dogged me as we passed, like I was gonna move in on their action. The men looked me up and down like I was the blue plate special. Hank grinned and shook his head, wrapping a protective arm around me. Like I needed to be protected from that sort of thing.

He led me past the DJ booth and more armed guards, then through double swinging doors into a different world.

The cavernous back room was unfinished, just concrete floors and exposed drywall, ghoulishly lit with buzzing fluorescent school-lunchroom fixtures. At the center of a circle of cheap folding chairs was a caged ring. In it, a thick, dark-skinned Mexican girl straddled and pummeled a bloody blonde ragdoll while a troll in a black and white striped shirt stood over them looking like he was about to take his dick out. Every seat would have been taken if the crowd weren't up on their feet howling and cheering in a cacophonous mix of Spanish and English.

Hank led me around behind the last row of seats. The concrete beneath our feet was mottled and stained and a sticky scatter of bloody feathers in the corners implied that humans weren't the only ones who fought in this room. We passed through a cheap blue plastic shower curtain hanging in a doorway and into a sort of makeshift holding area for fighters.

There were about six guys, two American and the rest Mexican. I recognized the Americans as students from the school. Hands were being wrapped and wounds stitched. Fighters stretched, sparred, and worked focus mitts. There was a heavy locker room funk, underscored by the hot penny smell of fresh blood.

"Wait here," Hank said. "I'm gonna go have me a little talk with Mr. Lovell."

He turned, taking a minute to slap shoulders and shake hands all around before slipping back out past the shower curtain.

Then, from a small closet-sized toilet in the back, there was Cody.

Shirtless, grinning, alive and unharmed. He wore fingerless gloves and loose knee-length black and red shorts slit high up the outside seam. As loose as they were, it still looked like he was trying to shoplift a Mexican papaya inside his athletic cup. He came over and hugged me like a long-lost best friend, holding on to me longer and tighter than was really necessary. I could feel that huge unyielding Tupperware container in his pants digging into my gut. He was a little sweaty and smelled faintly like a woman's perfume.

"Angel, wow, I'm so glad you made it." He pulled me back in for a second hug. "Is Hank with you?"

I nodded, frowning and pulling away.

"Are you okay?" I dropped my voice. "I thought those guys were gonna kill you."

He laughed, eyes way too bright.

"Nah, that was just a big misunderstanding. It's cool. Lovell just wanted to make sure I didn't leave town before the match tonight. He plays like he's all hard all the time, but he's really not a bad guy." He threw a couple of quick combinations in the air. "It sucks that this'll be my first fight that you get to watch. I'd much rather you get to see me kick some ass! Well, there's always next time, right?"

"But Cody," I asked as he bobbed and weaved, making me feel a bit seasick. "What about the missing supplements?"

"What are you talking about?" He stopped moving, eyebrows drawn together. "You mean the steroids? They aren't missing, I put them in the locker last night, just like always. Who told you about that anyway?"

I told him what the kid at the school told me.

"Aw, Beto's full of shit," Cody said. "Lovell didn't mention anything like that to me. Anyway, the steroids were just a side thing for extra money. I don't use that shit, I'm all natural. I have to be, y'know, for the show. Lovell's not even that pissed at me about the last fight. And you know what else, he told me he didn't have anything to do with what happened at the diner. He even joked about it, said if he wanted me killed, he'd do it right and I wouldn't be walking around like I am. Not that it's funny, what happened, I'm just saying. Anyway it's no big deal with Lovell. Everything's cool. It's just too bad you won't get to see me kick some ass."

He started up again with the lightning-fast combos while I started to feel a creeping cold sickness twisting in my belly.

"Cody," I asked. "Are you high?"

When he flashed that fucking Thick Vic smirk, I wanted to punch him in the face.

"Of course not, baby," Thick Vic said inside my head, just like he had a thousand times while we were together.

"Nah," Cody said. Then the smirk again. "Well maybe a little. It's no big deal. Lovell just had some girls over that wanted to party before the fight. It's not a problem or anything. It's really no big deal."

No big deal. Vic was dead, the same guys had tried to kill Cody, too, and suddenly the kid didn't seem to think anything was a big deal. I was starting to fear that all of this was, in fact, a very big deal. Something just didn't sit right about Cody's story. Not that I thought Cody was lying, but I felt sure there was more going on here than any of us knew. I didn't like that Lovell was giving Cody coke and the fact that the guys who shot Vic had been coked-up too made me wonder if Lovell really didn't have anything to do with the events at the diner.

Before I was able to voice any of this, a morose-looking Mexican with a stubbly gargoyle face stuck his head around the edge of the shower curtain.

"Noon y Guzman!" he called.

"I'm up," Cody said with a wink. "Catch you later."

As he walked away, I noticed the word OUTLAW was spelled out on the back of his shorts, mirroring the tattoo on his belly. I wondered what the hell I was thinking, coming here.

I didn't have an answer, so I followed Cody into the main room as the rowdy crowd cheered and whistled, chanting, *"Out-LAW! Out-LAW! Out-LAW!"*

Cody's opponent Guzman came out then, a tall, weedy kid with a fierce Conquistador's profile. The two of them entered the ring through a narrow door in the cage and the ref swiftly checked them both over, speaking to them in a voice too low to be heard above the howling crowd. Cody and Guzman touched gloves and then the fight began.

Both fighters came out cautious, circling. Cody seemed tightly wound and humming with aggressive energy while his opponent was more wary, hanging back and waiting for Cody to make the first move. After a series of feints and false starts, Cody finally let loose with a few fast, wildly aggressive punches and Guzman bobbed and weaved, countering. Cody ate a hard right that made the crowd hiss and whistle but he barely seemed to feel it. He lunged forward, shoulder aimed at Guzman's midsection and next thing I knew, Cody had lifted his opponent up over one shoulder and slammed him down on the mat.

Whatever they were doing down on the mat was hard for me to follow. I could barely see over the spectators' heads. When I could catch a glimpse, it looked like nothing much had happened, except that Cody was now sort of sideways on top rather than the missionary, belly-to-belly position he'd started out in.

I stopped watching the ring action and started looking through the crowd. I was surprised to see more American faces than Mexican. There were a lot of gorgeous women, and guys in expensive suits. There was some serious money flowing through this place.

A huge roar of excitement made me look back up at the ring. Cody was standing, hunched over and clutching his crotch. The ref didn't seem interested in this development, although even I, who knew virtually nothing about this sort of thing, was pretty sure that you weren't supposed to hit the other guy in the nuts. When Cody said no holds barred, I guess he wasn't kidding. Guzman was lying on his back with his bent legs in the air like he was waiting for a diaper change. Cody reacted to this indignity by kicking his downed opponent repeatedly, then dove in between Guzman's waving legs with an elbow to the face. I worried for a second that Cody had gone too far again, that maybe he just didn't have it in him to throw a fight. But instead of going in for the kill and finishing his stunned opponent, Cody backed off and gestured for Guzman to get up, playing the audience with broad, cocky showmanship that would have made Vic proud. He had that crowd eating out of his hand. In a way I was more impressed by this than his ability to execute complex grappling maneuvers. This, to me, said that Cody really did have what it took to be a star. If he managed to avoid whoever it was that wanted him dead.

Then a bell rang and the fighters were sent to their corners. I saw Hank step into the cage to assist Cody, so I figured the kid was in good hands.

On the far side of the ring, I noticed a small folding table with a locked cash box and a dry-erase board full of fight stats, matchups and odds. A mannish Mexican cougar in a low-cut black dress sat behind the table ignoring the action in the ring and reading a small, square romance comic book. There was another guard with an AK47 beside and slightly behind her, either trying to look down her cleavage or trying to read over her shoulder. Clearly the betting was closed now that the fights were on.

On the other side of the betting table were two doors. One was closed and marked *Private*. The other was open and led to a small storage area. From where I stood, I could see stacks of identical cardboard boxes inside.

When I moved casually around to the other side of the open doorway, I could read the labels on the boxes. *UltraSalud: Proteína de Soya*. My Spanish wasn't great, but that had to mean soy protein. These had to be the infamous supplements. I decided I needed a closer look.

The bell rang and the fight resumed. Cody immediately shot in with another showy takedown. The armed guard looked up from the cougar's cleavage, stretching up on his toes to see over the heads of the standing audience, and I swiftly slipped in through the open doorway before I could think about what an astoundingly bad idea it was.

Inside the small storage room, the boxes were stacked higher than my head, but one box sat over on the far side by itself. It had obviously been opened and re-sealed with different tape. I squatted down beside it, picked a corner of the cheap tape loose and peeled the box open.

Inside, jars of protein powder, vanilla flavor. I pulled one out, cracked it open and shook it, tasting the vanilla dust on my lips. It seemed to contain what it claimed to contain. I took a moment to make sure no one had noticed me, then dipped my fingers into the jar, combing blindly through the powder. I shook the jar again and dug under the surface of the stuff until my fingertips hit paydirt.

Now I'm no expert on steroids, but I'm pretty sure that the stuff comes either in the form of a pill or an injectable liquid. I'm positive that it doesn't come powdered and tightly packed into white bricks wrapped up in clear plastic.

I wasn't looking at steroids. I was looking at cocaine.

16.

I stuck the brick of coke back into the wide-mouthed jar and shoved the protein powder back over it. I was screwing the lid back on when I felt the cold snout of a gun against the back of my neck.

"Up," someone said. I assumed it was probably the armed guard from the betting table but was too scared to look back. I stood up.

The guy stripped my go-bag off my shoulder and gripped my arm, leading me out of the supply closet and into the room marked *Private*.

Finally, Mr. Lovell.

He looked nothing like I expected. I don't even know what I was expecting, but I certainly wasn't expecting Nick Manning's cowboy brother.

Lovell had that same half-up, half-down shoulder-length hairstyle that Nick sported during the height of his career "dropping loads" on the adult industry. Lovell also had a similar long, handsome face, but his eyes were dark and flat. He wore a black-on-black western-style suit with narrow, glossy leather lapels and onyx buttons that matched his onyx bolo tie. There was a black cowboy hat sitting on the desk. Anyone else wearing that kind of over-the-top western fetish get-up would have come off way more camp and sleazy, but this guy seemed chilly and soulless, like a mannequin being used to display the clothing of a dead country-western singer. There was something oddly ageless about him. He could have been thirty or sixty or anywhere in between.

"Who is this?" he asked the guard, like I was a piece of junk mail. I was expecting a Southern accent, based on the fancy cowboy drag, but his deep voice was as bland and generic as a newscaster's.

"Don't know," the guard said with only the lightest Mexican accent. "She was messing with the shipment."

From the other side of the door, came a massive wave of hoots and whistles.

"I don't have time to deal with this now," Lovell said. "My hands are full with this Cody situation."

He picked up a walkie-talkie from his immaculate desk.

"Am I happy?" Lovell asked.

"He tapped," replied a crackly, disembodied voice.

Lovell nodded.

"Good boy. I want him in this office as soon as he's out of the ring."

"You got it," the voice said.

"What do you want me to do about her?" the guard asked, poking me again with the rifle.

He turned and looked at me without blinking.

"She'll just have to wait."

What the hell else was I gonna do? I waited.

The little office was hot and stuffy, even with a small, noisy air conditioner running full blast. My pal with the gun was sweating through his cheap cologne and the resulting olfactory experience was less than pleasant. Lovell sat down behind his desk and waited without moving, like a stonefish.

When a knock sounded on the door, my pal with the gun was so startled, I was afraid he was gonna shoot me.

"Come on in," Lovell said, placing his palms flat on the desk.

It was Cody, escorted by a huge Mexican biker with a thinning ponytail. Cody had changed from his fight gear into track pants and a t-shirt that read HAYABUSA and featured the silhouette of a flying bird against a red sun. He had a towel around his sweaty neck and his handsome face seemed shiny and unevenly swollen, eyes squeezed down to slits. His big hands were red and wrinkled from being under tight wraps and gloves.

When Cody walked into the room, something happened to Lovell that I would not have believed if I hadn't seen it with my own eyes. His cold blank face flushed pink, spilt wide by a big, friendly smile. It was as if someone had flipped the humanity switch behind his eyes.

"Cody," he said. "Fantastic."

"What's up?" Cody asked. Then he turned and noticed me. "Oh hey, Angel." He paused and did a double take when he saw my pal with the rifle. He turned back to Lovell, brow creased. "Um…"

Lovell nodded to the meathead, who grabbed Cody's arms and held them behind his back.

"Whoa, hey," Cody said. "What the fuck?"

Lovell came out from behind his desk with a compact nine in his hand. He pressed the barrel to Cody's forehead, making his eyes cross. Lovell was still smiling.

"What the fuck?" Cody was saying again. "I did just like you said!"

Lovell lowered the gun, slapped Cody lightly several times on the cheek and shook his head like an indulgent uncle.

"Cody, Cody, Cody," he said, gun still pointed in Cody's general direction. "You're breaking my heart right now. You know you are."

"What…" Cody said. "But I…" He turned to me, fear and anguish in his eyes. "Angel…"

"This your woman?" Lovell asked gesturing towards me with the gun.

"No," Cody shook his head. "No, I mean, she's just a friend. But…"

"A friend you sent to steal from me?" Lovell asked. "Haven't you stolen enough from me already?"

Cody looked at me, then back at Lovell. "I don't understand."

I was watching Cody's face this whole time, trying to get a read. He was either the best actor on earth or he had absolutely no idea what this was about.

"He had nothing to do with that," I said. "I wasn't gonna take anything, I was just being nosy."

"Nosy?" Lovell turned that awful smile towards me and it made me wish I'd kept my mouth shut. "And was it also you who was nosy in Cody's locker this morning?"

Lovell came over to me and pressed the muzzle of his gun against my sternum, eyebrows raised in mild curiosity.

I had my nipples pierced back in the mid-nineties. Got sick of the rings after about five years and took them out, but that's not the point.

See, when the needle went through the first time, it was shocking, like lightning. The pain was intense and sudden and astounding and then the ring was in and my heart was racing and I thought, *Wow, I did it. It's over*. Then the piercer started prepping the other nipple.

That second nipple was a thousand times worse. The first time I had no similar experience to compare it to, no idea what was coming, but that second time. That second time every single nerve in my body knew exactly what was coming. That was the worst pain I had ever experienced. Well, before the whole vigilante thing, anyway.

What I'm trying to say is this. When Lovell asked if I had his missing cocaine, I flashed back hard to another man asking about something that was missing. Torturing me. Suddenly, any semblance of bad-ass I might have cultivated since then went right out the window. People who think they'd be all tough in that kind of situation have never been really hurt.

"Leave her alone," Cody said, trying to be valiant, struggling against the meathead's grip. "She didn't do anything."

"So you admit it was you?" Lovell asked.

"What was me?" Cody asked, voice cracking. "What the fuck are you talking about?" Then suddenly, realization flooded his features. "Okay, hang on a second. You're saying something *was* missing from the shipment?"

"Yes," Lovell said. "That's what I'm saying."

"Why the fuck would I want to steal steroids?" he asked. "You know I can't use that shit because of the show. It must have been Beto, or someone else from the school."

"Steroids." Lovell squinted at Cody. "Right. Who else has the combination for your locker?"

"Well..." Cody paused, brow creased. "Well, nobody except your pick-up guy. How do you know he didn't take it?"

"Because I know," Lovell said. "Just like I know it was you who took the missing jar."

"I didn't take anything," Cody said. "You're crazy."

Lovell froze, genial smile melting away.

"Okay," he said. "I'm done with this now."

He turned away from us and stood there, unmoving, while the biker bound Cody's hands behind his back with a length of greasy, splintery rope. I'm ashamed to admit the tremendous, knee-melting relief I felt when it became evident that Lovell wasn't going to torture me. At least not right then and there.

"Mr. Lovell, listen," Cody said. "This is some kind of terrible misunderstanding, okay? Come on, can't we just talk about this for a second?"

The biker stuck a knotted rag in Cody's mouth and tied it behind his head. Apparently not.

"I'm writing this off," Lovell said to no one in particular as he sat down behind his desk.

"Let's go, baby," my pal with the gun said to me, gripping my upper arm and hustling me out of the office. Cody and the biker followed close behind.

Out in the main room with the ring nobody noticed or cared about us as we were marched along behind the last row of seats. They were all too into the fight. When I looked up into the ring, I saw it was Hank up there.

His face was flushed, lips distended and horsey from his mouthguard. One eye was bloody and swollen shut, but he seemed to notice me right at the same moment that I noticed him. His head turned, good eye widening at the sight of the guy with the rifle behind me. Hank's handsome Mexican opponent took that split-second distraction to deliver a devastating right that sent Hank spinning across the ring in a drunken pirouette. The crowd screamed and jeered and the guy with the rifle steered me away, towards a large metal fire door in the back of the room. I stole one last glance at the ring, and saw Hank face down on the mat with the ref crouching over him waving his arms. I was horribly sure that was going to be the last time I ever saw Hank.

17.

The fire door led to a fenced-in parking lot. A dented blue-and-white '70s-era Suburban was idling just outside the door like it had been waiting for us. Behind the wheel was an older guy with slick white hair and a stoic Indio face. He nodded, then got out, spat on the concrete and headed around to unlock the hatchback.

The biker brought Cody forward, bound his ankles together and tossed him into the back of the Suburban like a trussed buck. The white-haired guy got back behind the wheel and for a second I was sure he was gonna drive off with Cody and that would be that. I even had a half-composed apology to Vic spinning through my mind when my pal with the rifle dragged me over to the passenger side, threw my go-bag in and got in after it, then pulled me up into his lap.

I tried to shut out my fear and anger and how bad I wanted to break the guy's wandering fingers as they kept on finding their way up under my shirt. I tried to focus and think of nothing but how close that go-bag was, bumping against my foot as the big old SUV tore down winding, unpaved roads to God only knew where. My pal had the long rifle at his side, but there wasn't enough space for him to actually use it. He and the driver were having some kind of spirited debate in Spanish. There had to be a way to get to the tiny Warthog in the side pocket of my go-bag, but I didn't want to give even the smallest hint that I was anything other than a terrified little girl until I was sure I could prove it.

As we drove, I pictured Cody in the back, bound and bouncing painfully around. What could be going through his mind? Was he really as clueless as he seemed? He seemed to really believe this was all about steroids. Or at least that's what he wanted me to think. He had evidently inherited his father's taste for narcotics. No reason he couldn't also have inherited Vic's ability to lie to my face with earnest, heartfelt conviction.

I wanted to believe Cody. I *needed* to believe him if I was going to keep on sticking my neck out to save his ass, but if I was honest with myself, I had to admit that I wasn't entirely convinced he was on the level.

Before I could come up with some way to get my hand on the Warthog, we abruptly arrived at wherever we were going. The driver slowed, pulled the Suburban over. The debate raged on as they both got out and dragged me out with them. We were nowhere, a particular kind of barren, empty desert nowhere that I was unfortunately quite familiar with. The kind of nowhere where you brought people who wouldn't be coming back.

My pal with the rifle was getting increasingly handsy, tugging at my breasts and gripping my ass. It was becoming obvious that the debate was about whether or not fucking me first would be a good idea. Not that I had any desire to fuck that guy, but I was still less than thrilled when he apparently lost the argument. It just meant they were going to get on with the killing that much quicker, giving me even less time to figure a way out of this.

The white-haired guy muscled Cody out of the back of the

Suburban and untied his ankles so he could walk, marching him away from the car at the end of a small revolver while the other guy grabbed a shovel and handed it to me.

"Dig," he said, pointing with his rifle to a sandy patch of dirt about fifty feet from the front bumper of the car.

I looked over at Cody. He was pale and sweating, eyes huge and chin slick with drool from the gag. He was shaking his head from side to side and making lots of emphatic *mmmmphs* through the cloth. There was no way I was gonna let it end like this. I gripped the shovel hard and thought about using it for something other than digging. I knew I would only get one chance.

I started digging to buy myself some time. The guy with the rifle was to my left and slightly closer than Cody and the driver to my right. I figured I had at least an hour, probably more since I was going at it alone. That kind of monotonous hard labor leaves the brain wide open for figuring and I could feel something like a plan beginning to form.

I could see that my pal with the rifle was getting bored. He was trying to stay threatening, but I kept on catching him staring off into the night sky or kicking at pebbles like an impatient child. At that point I was standing nearly waist deep in the growing hole and I decided it was time.

I started slowing down, breathing heavily and acting like the shovel was too heavy to lift. Like the work had worn me out and I was nearing exhaustion. My pal was barely paying attention. My muscles felt shaky, stomach sick with adrenaline as I sucked in a deep, dusty breath and then collapsed in what I hoped was a cute, girly faint.

I heard my pal swear softly and then the crunch of his

footsteps towards the edge of the hole. I lay flat on my back at the bottom with the shovel clutched to my chest. I could feel a startled insect crawling across my neck but I didn't move to swat at it. I waited.

He knelt down to haul me up, and when the oval of his head appeared over the edge of the hole I let him have it with the shovel.

I was up on my feet in a heartbeat, following through with a second and third crack with the blade of the shovel, laying the bastard out on the sand.

I was expecting the driver to start shooting at any moment and was ready to dive back in the hole, but when I turned to him, I saw him lying curled up on the ground with Cody kicking the shit out of him. Clearly Cody didn't need his hands. All he had needed was a split-second distraction to kick the revolver over to where it now lay, beside a smooth flat rock about ten feet away. In that moment I was ready to forgive Cody for any and everything he might have done to get us into this situation in the first place.

I let my pal have one more from the shovel, grabbed the fallen rifle and then ran to where Cody stood over the driver. The older man was out cold, drooling blood into the sand. Meanwhile my pal was trying to get up on his knees, one hand pressed to his bleeding nose. I wanted to untie Cody and pull out his gag, but my hands were full with the rifle and the shovel and there just wasn't time.

"Let's get the hell out of here before they get up," I said.

Cody nodded and we ran together to the Suburban. I dropped the shovel but not the rifle and then dove into the driver's seat, hand reaching for the ignition.

No keys.

"Shit," I said, climbing back out of the Suburban. "The driver must have the keys."

Cody, still bound and gagged, *mmphed* loudly, eyes wide and frantically gesturing with his chin towards the downed men.

"What?" I asked, raising one hand to remove the gag.

He kicked me hard in the back of my knees, causing them to buckle. I fell awkwardly backward onto the rough sand, a curse half formed in my mouth. But just before I hit, the crack of a small-caliber shot echoed through the jagged rocks and arroyos.

I rolled under the Suburban, clutching the rifle to my chest. I couldn't see where Cody had gone, but I didn't see him dead on the ground either, so I figured he must still be on his feet somewhere behind the Suburban.

Another pop and I raised myself up on my elbows, set the rifle on semi and aimed in the direction of the noise, sending out a silent thank you to Duncan's ghost for everything he'd taught me about the venerable old Kalashnikov.

From what I'd seen, the driver was down for the count, but the guy I'd hit with the shovel seemed to be more resilient. It had to be him shooting at us. I scanned the darkness, spotted a low, creeping shape crowned with bloody white hair. The driver was moving, trying to crawl away. I still didn't think he was up for a gunfight. I pointed the rifle towards the last place I'd seen the bigger guy and pulled the trigger, hoping to make him give himself away. It worked. The revolver replied with another shot that hit the dirt beside the large front tire a few feet to my left and the muzzle flash caught my eye. The bastard was down in the hole I'd dug.

"Cody!" I called. "If you can hear me, make a run for the keys. I'll cover you."

I fired again in the direction of the hole. I had the clear advantage with the rifle, but the big guy would only need one lucky shot to take Cody out. I was tempted to flip to full auto and make with the lead firehose. That would definitely keep the guy down for a few scary seconds, probably make him piss his pants too, but I didn't want to blow my whole wad all at once. Cody would need more time. My hands were sweaty, shaking.

I saw a flash of Cody making the run for the driver and I covered him with a dozen quick but controlled shots. I wasn't watching Cody. I was staring at the hole, trying to will my night vision to sharpen. I hoped the pause would tempt the big guy to peek up.

I let my gaze flick to Cody and saw him crouched backward beside the driver, feeling blindly inside the guy's jacket, head tipped up to the starry sky.

A swift blur of movement drew my eye back to the hole and I pulled the trigger. I'm hardly a crack shot, so I didn't think I got a good hit, but I must have at least grazed him, because he yelped and swore like he'd been stung by a bee.

When I looked at Cody he was running towards the Suburban. I couldn't tell if he had the keys or not. I crawled out from under the car and fired off another dozen to cover Cody's retreat, but the big guy was too smart to pop up again.

Cody loudly jingled the keys he held behind his back and then ducked into the car. I followed, sliding into the driver's seat and tossing the rifle into the rear. Cody leaned forward, twisting his hands towards me. I took the keys, slid them into the ignition and cranked it.

As I hit the gas and pulled away in a spray of gravel, Cody's window shattered and my heart nearly stopped. I was expecting to turn and see him shot in the face, bleeding and dying, but he was fine. Gagged and terrified but fine, unharmed. There was a large, fist-sized rock on the seat beside him. We both looked down at the rock, and then up at each other.

Another loud clunk from the rear and I looked in the mirror to see the big guy running after the Suburban, winging rocks like a major league pitcher. Man, was he pissed. I sped up and out of range and his angry face faded into the darkness.

18.

I kept the pedal to the metal for another five or ten minutes. When I came to a crossroads, I pulled the car over, figuring I ought to stop driving in a random, headlong panic and figure out where we should be going. See if there was a map in the glove box. My heart was still pounding, hands shaking so badly I thought I might rip the wheel right off the steering column. There was a small wooden cross stuck in the dirt about ten feet ahead, wreathed with dusty plastic flowers. It was the only visible human structure. No houses or buildings for miles. Nobody in sight.

I turned to look at Cody. His face was flushed, eyes wide. He just sat there for a moment, still and silent, then started laughing behind his gag. I shook my head and leaned over to untie his hands.

When they were free, he pulled off the gag, smacked his palms against the dashboard and whooped like a rabid sports fan. He tore the passenger door open and tumbled out, laughing and howling at the moon with his arms spread wide.

I left the Suburban running and managed to open my own door, got my shaky legs under me and stepped out onto the rocky shoulder. I felt like a newborn giraffe. Cody's laughter was contagious.

"Jesus," he said with another wild laugh. "Did you see that guy's face? Fuck, I can't believe we're alive."

"Believe it," I said, laughing too.

He grabbed my wrists and whirled me around.

"You were awesome," he said, stopping and holding both my hands. "Seriously. Do you do this kind of thing a lot?"

"No," I said. "I try to avoid this kind of thing."

He looked down at me, his eyes in shadow, nothing visible but the bright pinpoints of reflected headlights. Then he slipped an arm around my waist and pulled me into another one of his intense, full-body hugs. This time, he wouldn't let me go and suddenly everything was different.

I could feel that big Pagliuca dick waking up under his track pants, sliding against my hip. He was breathing too fast, hands sweaty against the small of my back.

The next thing I knew, we were making out.

After a few endless, drowning minutes, I pulled away, trying to catch my breath and keep my wits about me.

"Okay," I said. "Okay, hang on a second."

I reached back into the car to grab the last rubber from a pocket in my go-bag.

"Here," I said, tossing him the little plastic packet.

"Sure, yeah," he said, tearing it open with his teeth while I got my shorts and panties off over my shoes.

I watched him struggle heroically to get the condom on for nearly a minute before it finally tore and snapped into two pieces, leaving behind a comically tight ring of rubber about halfway down. I should have just put it on with my mouth.

"Shit," he swore, ripping off the torn remnant and throwing it into the dust. "Sorry. Have you got another one?"

I shook my head.

"Fuck," he said.

He just stood there for a moment, head down and unsure but still hard. I'm not proud of what I did next.

"Fuck it," I said.

Now you got to understand, I haven't had unprotected sex since before Cody was born. It was all kinds of wrong, but goddamn it was good. The kid was ravenous, on fire, and he popped like the fourth of July after less than a minute inside me, but he kept on going without missing a beat. Another classic Thick Vic move. In his prime, Vic had been famous for delivering two or three high volume pop shots in one scene without breaking his stride. Even though he lacked Vic's experience and finesse, Cody was clearly his father's son.

I wasn't all that worried about getting knocked up, since I'd had several nasty bouts of Pelvic Inflammatory Disease in my reckless youth and had been told by my gyno that I'd probably never be able to have kids. Besides, at this rate if I lived long enough to need to worry about pregnancy or STDs, I'd consider myself lucky. For the next twenty minutes, I didn't think about anything other than how good it felt to be alive.

Then, suddenly, I found myself thinking about Hank and the way his body had pressed up against mine as he twisted me around on the mat. About how bad I wanted to take control of that powerful, dangerous body and push it to its limits. Drive it like a racecar. I was right on the edge and thinking about Hank put me over, hard.

After that, I found myself thinking about Vic again, about him asking me to take care of Cody. About him dying. I started to feel weird about fucking his kid. About the fact that Cody was young enough to be *my* son. At that point, I just wanted to put an end to it, so I flipped the switch in my head to pro mode. I pulled away and bent down to finish him off with my mouth.

"Fuck!" Cody said when I was done, the curse drawn out long and incredulous. "That was amazing."

I chuckled under my breath. At least he didn't say *awesome*.

He made a grab for me like he meant to pull me in for another make-out session, but I dodged out of range and started hunting around for my panties. I found them crumpled and filthy by the Suburban's front tire so I tossed them aside and put my shorts on without them.

"I've never met a girl that could go all the way down on me like that," he said, stuffing his dick back into his pants. "That was seriously the most amazing blow job of all time."

"Glad you enjoyed it kid," I replied. "Because it's never gonna happen again."

"Damn," he said. "I was just about to ask you to marry me."

I shook my head and walked back around to the driver's side.

"Look in the glovebox," I told him as I opened the door and slid back into the driver's seat. "See if you can find a map so we can figure out where the hell we are."

19.

It turned out there was no map anywhere in the Suburban, so we picked the direction that seemed the most likely to be north-ish and headed down that road. Cody fell asleep in the passenger seat almost instantly, leaving me alone with my jangling, disjointed thoughts.

An hour later, we simply ran out of road.

It was impossible to tell if the road builders had just lost interest or if the desert had swallowed the road under smooth shifting sand, but for whatever reason, we had hit a dead end. The gas gauge in the Suburban was getting dangerously low. I found a two-liter Coke bottle under the driver's seat that was half full of what turned out to be some kind of slimy, rotgut liquor, but there was no water. I was exhausted now that the manic adrenaline had drained away. Dawn was creeping around under the edge of the sky, flushing the distant mountains a feverish pink. Soon it would be very hot.

It seemed like some kind of awful joke. I'd survived so many human killers, but now, in this modern era of GPS and smartphones, I was lost in the Mexican desert without food or water. Of all the ways I'd thought I might die, this was definitely not one of them.

Of course, at least one of the guys who were supposed to kill and bury us was out there somewhere, still alive and presumably still pissed. Unlike us, he probably did have a phone and friends to come get him. He also knew the area way better than we did and could be driving down the road towards us right now. We might not get the chance to die of exposure after all.

"Wake up, kid," I said to Cody.

Cody stirred in the passenger seat, rubbing his squinty eyes.

"Where the hell are we?" he asked.

"No idea," I said. "I'll tell you what I do know, though. We probably don't have enough gas to make it back to the crossroads where we started."

"I saw a gas can in the back," Cody said. "Bumped my head on it a few times and it didn't feel empty."

"Thank fucking God," I said.

I tossed Cody the keys. He hopped out and went around back to open the hatch. I looked into the rear-view mirror and saw him holding up a dented red metal gas can in one hand and giving me a thumbs-up with the other. He used the can to fill the tank while I sat there and struggled to keep my eyes open.

I got out to stretch my sore muscles and decided to ditch the rifle. We had enough potential problems facing us at the border without trying to smuggle an automatic rifle into the States. I stuck the thing nose first into the sand and left it there like some kind of corny political statement. Of course I still had my two handguns, but there was no way I was gonna get rid of those. That was a chance I'd just have to take.

I came around the Suburban to where Cody stood with the empty gas can.

"I have to ask you something important," I said.

"Sure," he replied.

"I'm not here to judge you or tell you what to do," I said.

"And I'm still gonna help you no matter what you say, but I need to know the truth. Did you take Lovell's cocaine?"

"Sure, a little," he said, eyebrows hunched together. "Just a couple of lines when I was over at his house, but I already told you that."

"That's not what I meant," I said. "I meant did you steal the missing jar from Lovell's shipment."

He squinted at me. "You mean the steroids?"

"I looked inside those jars," I said. "They were filled with bricks of cocaine, not steroids. You're telling me you really didn't know that?"

"Seriously?" he asked. "Are you sure? I mean, did you taste it?"

"Cody, don't fuck with me," I said.

"I'm not!" He looked hurt and genuinely puzzled. "I just… I mean… Fuck."

"So you had no idea?" I asked. "Look me in the eyes and tell me that."

"Jesus, Angel," he said, eyes locked on mine. "I had no idea. Why would I lie about something like that?"

I studied his face, knowing that if he was as good a liar as his father, I would probably never know the truth.

"Okay, fine," I said. "I'm beat. You drive."

He smiled.

"Sure, baby," he said. "Bend over."

I rolled my eyes and got into the passenger seat. I took a lightweight hoodie out of my go-bag, put it on and pulled the hood down over my eyes. I was out before Cody got back into the car.

It took the better part of the day to find our way back

to the border, but thanks to Cody's broad pantomime and shameless pidgin Spanglish, he was able to charm fairly accurate directions out of a group of amused prostitutes outside a shabby little roadhouse that got us pointed in the right direction. No sign of Lovell's guys. At one point, I tried halfheartedly to convince Cody that we should head in the other direction. Not return to the U.S. at all. It made way more sense, what with all the various people who wanted one or both of us dead, but Cody was having none of it. Nothing mattered to the kid besides being in Vegas at 8 AM Sunday morning for his big television debut on *All American Fighter*. It was dark by the time we made the border.

The extremely tan, extremely fit blonde woman at the border took my brand-new passport, held it up to the light and stared at it for way too long. Her eye bounced from my face to the photo and back again over and over and when she called one of her fellow guards to come look at it, too, I was sure the gig was up.

She let me sweat for nearly a minute. Cody was getting antsy and short-tempered. I was afraid he was going to start complaining and making a scene. He had no idea my passport was fake. No idea how close we were to fucked.

Then she handed the passport back to me and motioned for us to drive through.

"What the hell was that about?" Cody asked after a while.

"No idea," I said. Then: "Look, we need to get rid of this car."

"Fine," Cody said. "But first I need to stop at my place."

"Absolutely not." I shook my head. "No. No way. That's a terrible idea."

I didn't mention that I wanted to go back to Hank's, to make sure that he was okay. I knew that was a terrible idea too but it didn't stop me from wanting to do it.

"I'm sorry," Cody said. "I can drop you somewhere first if you want me to, but I have to check on my mom. She gets… I just need to check on her."

After all this, there was no way I was gonna let the kid out of my sight. I'd promised Vic, and while I wasn't planning on being Cody's pistol-packing fairy godmother for the rest of my life, I'd gotten it into my head that if I just got him to Vegas, got him on that damn show, I'd be off the hook. No one would kill him while he was on camera, and the way he'd described it, the cameras were rolling 24/7. I could walk away feeling that I'd fulfilled Vic's dying request. But at the moment, Vegas seemed so far away.

Cody's house was in a rough, seedy neighborhood full of trailers, pit bull breeders and meth labs. It was a scabby little L-shaped house with heavy bars on all the windows, distinguished from its neighbors only by the fact that it didn't have multiple broken-down cars parked around it. The one car in the driveway was a small, sad import with a smashed headlight. The yard was mostly bare rocky dirt and a few brown, dying cacti. I marveled at what a bad gardener you had to be to kill cacti.

I made Cody drive by twice to make sure there was nobody lying in wait for us. It looked clear but I still took the Warthog out of my bag and slipped it into the pocket of my hoodie. Cody parked and got out. I followed but stayed wary, hackles up and trying to grow eyes in the back of my head. Nothing. Nothing that I could see, anyway. It was dark, just after 9 PM.

Cody unlocked the front door and motioned for me to enter. Inside, there was a weird unclean, spoiled milk smell beneath a cover of cloying fake flower air freshener. The dark blue carpet was worn thin but recently vacuumed. The furniture was mostly cheap and tacky except for a ridiculously expensive black leather recliner, the kind with drink holders and built in shiatsu and more control buttons than the space shuttle. There was also a brand new Xbox and a huge flat screen television, on with the sound turned down. Lovell's money no doubt. I suddenly wanted to ask Cody again if he'd taken Lovell's coke and probably would have if I hadn't noticed Hank sitting in the leather recliner, holding his revolver in his lap.

"Hank!" Cody cried, flinging himself at him and throwing his arms around his chest. "God I'm glad to see you!"

I was a little embarrassed by how glad I was to see Hank too, but something didn't feel right about this so I hung back and held my tongue.

After Cody let him go, Hank just sat there silent for a minute, looking down at the gun. Then, he spoke.

"Y'all had better sit down," he said.

Cody dropped down on the sofa, face creased with concern. I sat beside him, liking this even less.

"Is everything okay?" Cody asked. He bounced back up to his feet, panic in his voice. "Is it Mom? Is she okay?"

"She's fine," Hank said. "Would you just sit down for a second?"

"Sorry," Cody said. He sat again. "What is it?"

"It's like this," Hank said and then trailed off.

He paused for a long time as if he were considering how to say what needed to be said. When he finally spoke up again, I understood why.

"Cody," he said. "Lovell sent me here to kill you."

20.

I put my hand in my pocket, wrapping my fingers around the stubby grip of the Warthog, holding my breath without even realizing I was doing it. Cody laughed, forced and too loud, then fell silent.

"You're kidding, right?" he asked.

Hank shook his head ruefully.

"I wish I was," Hank said.

"Yeah, but…" Cody frowned. "I mean…you're not really gonna do it. Are you?"

Hank didn't answer right away. I could feel the cold, speedy adrenaline flooding though my exhausted body, but I wasn't sure if I could keep it up anymore.

"Been sitting here thinking on it for some time now," Hank said, looking back down at the gun. "And I came to the conclusion that I ain't. I can't. It's that simple. Reckon he's gonna kill me if I don't. But the way I see it, it's a fair trade."

"What?" Cody said. "What are you talking about? That's crazy!"

"You got your whole career ahead of you." Hank said. "I got nothing."

"Jesus," Cody said. "Hank, don't talk like that. You have us, right? Me and Angel." He turned, including me with a desperate gesture. "Besides, I need you in my corner if I'm gonna make it in the AAFC. I can't do it without you!"

"Sure you can," Hank said. "You'll have Matt Kenner.

He's twice the fighter I ever was and he don't get mixed up and forget things half the time the way I do."

"Bullshit!" Cody said. "No, this is bullshit, I'm not buying this. There has to be another way."

"You'd best get on the road," Hank said. "I done talked to Mrs. Dean next door about looking in on your momma. You got nothing to worry about now except getting to Vegas." Hank turned to me, something unreadable in his expression. "I'm sorry to put this on you, Angel, but I reckon it's up to you to keep an eye on the kid from here on out." He smiled and all it did was make his hard, ugly face seem even more resigned. "I know he's in good hands."

I had just about had it with doomed men asking me to take care of Cody.

"It doesn't have to end like this, Hank," I said. "Come with us. We can stay ahead of Lovell but we need you. I can't do this alone."

"I don't think…" Hank began, but Cody cut him off.

"You have to come, Hank," Cody said. "It's like Angel says, we can't make it without you. You have to help us!"

"I don't know," he said, but I could see he was losing his resolve.

Cody stood, grabbed Hank by the wrist and pulled him to his feet.

"Look, it's decided. You're coming."

"You ain't gonna let this go are you?" Hank asked.

"Nope," Cody replied, grinning like he'd already won.

"Cody?" a thin, quavering and ancient-sounding voice called out from the other side of the room.

When I turned, I was expecting a little old lady. What I

saw was Cody's mother. Skye West. Or, should I say, a person that used to be Skye West.

If I had not known it was her, I never would have recognized her. Back in the day she was willowy and sweet-faced, a freckled little hippie nymph with wavy, naturally blond hair, big green eyes and a perpetually stoned smile. Now she was not so much overweight as swollen, her face puffy and pale and her formerly lithe body doughy and shapeless as a stuffed laundry bag. Her colorless hair was cut short and thinning and she wore faded sweatpants and a stained t-shirt. She moved towards Cody with a slow, medicated shuffle.

"Mom," Cody said. "Mom, is everything okay?"

"I heard talking," she said, eyeing me suspiciously.

"That was just me and Hank," Cody said, taking her hands. "Mom, why won't you wear any of the nice new dresses I bought you?"

"Who's that?" she asked, tipping her chin towards me, eyes gone narrow and fearful. She didn't seem to recognize me.

"That's my friend Angel," Cody said and I immediately wished he hadn't.

Skye looked me over, studying me like there was gonna be a test. I waited for the fireworks, but amazingly, they never came.

"Hank is here," she told Cody.

"I know, Mom," Cody said. "I see him."

"He said you're leaving me," she said, suddenly petulant as a child.

"I just have to go to Vegas for a little while," Cody said. "But Shelley Dean is gonna come by every day to check on you and make sure you eat and don't forget to take your meds. I'll call whenever I can and by the time I come back I'll have so much money I'll be able to buy you a new house and a new car. What kind of car do you want? A Porsche?"

"You *are* leaving!" she wailed. "I knew it!"

"Okay, Mom, don't cry." He put his arm around her and then stage whispered over his shoulder to me and Hank. "Just give me a minute."

He led his mother out of the room, speaking softly to her as they went. I stood with Hank, waiting. Hank didn't speak, he just held his gun at his side and looked at his feet. I was hit again with how glad I was to see him, and that he'd agreed to come with us. I had no clue what was wrong with me, or how I'd managed to get so crushed out on a guy who might as well have *bad idea* tattooed on his forehead. But after my ill-advised quickie with Cody, it seemed like I was on a roll in the bad idea department.

I looked over at the television, hoping for distraction. An ad for something I didn't need. Then local news. The first thing up, a photo of Duncan's Diner, followed by a sketch some police artist had done of me. With the sound off, I had no idea what they were saying about me, but I didn't really need to know. The fact that my face was on television for any reason was the worst possible development. I had to assume the Croatians who were after me had seen this too. If they weren't here already, they were definitely on the way. As if there weren't already enough reasons to get the hell out of Yuma.

Thankfully, Cody picked that moment to come back. Over one shoulder he had a black and red duffle bag printed with a logo so spiky that I couldn't read it.

"She gonna be okay?" Hank asked Cody.

"I hope so," Cody said. He looked back over his shoulder at the closed door like he wasn't so sure. "You know how I worry about her, Hank, but I can't stay here and take care of her forever. I have to live my own life. Right?"

" 'Course you do," Hank said. "Now let's get out of here before I go and change my mind."

"Yeah, okay," Cody said.

Cody walked over to the front door and opened it. Standing on the other side of the doorway was the horny toad in the cowboy hat and his large Native American friend. Behind them, black hat pulled down low over his eyes, was Mr. Lovell.

21.

The horny toad had a pistol in his hand and jammed the muzzle into Cody's belly, backing him up into the house. The big guy stepped aside to let Lovell enter, then came inside himself, closing the door and standing in front of it like a bouncer.

"I'm not surprised by your actions, Hank," Lovell said. "Just deeply disappointed."

"Well, I'd be glad to tell you what you can do with your disappointment, Vernon," Hank said. "But I won't on account of there being a lady present."

"Guns," the horny toad said. "Let's have 'em."

Hank tossed his revolver on the carpet at the horny toad's feet. I did the same with the Warthog, but figured I'd keep my go-bag on my shoulder until they specifically asked me to do otherwise. The Sig was in an inner pocket, and I could feel its weight against the small of my back, but I didn't have any idea how to reach it without attracting attention.

The toad scooped up the guns and pocketed them both.

"Kill the woman first," Lovell said.

I was about to make that grab for the Sig and to hell with the consequences, but I saw over the toad's shoulder that Cody's mom had drifted back into the room.

"Cody?" she said, her voice tiny. "I thought you left. I..."

Everyone in the room turned towards her as she raised

her hand and opened it to reveal an empty prescription pill bottle. The inside of her arm was sliced open from her wrist to her elbow. The pill bottle rolled off her palm and fell to the carpet.

I took advantage of the distraction to pull the Sig and point it at Lovell.

"Mom!" Cody made a lunge towards her but the toad gripped his shirt, shoving his pistol up under Cody's chin.

"Take it easy now, Cody," the toad said. "And you—" He gestured at me. "Drop the gun."

Cody's mom took a halting step forward, staggered and fell to her knees.

"Get the fuck off me," Cody cried, twisting frantically in his grip.

"Tell your boy to let Cody go," I said to Lovell.

"Forget it," Lovell said, staring me down without flinching. "You pull that trigger and the boy dies with me."

"Jesus, Mom," Cody said. "Somebody call 911!"

"Nobody's calling anyone," Lovell said.

Hank knelt down beside Skye, pulled his shirt off and wrapped it around her forearm.

"Hang on now, Ms. Noon," Hank said.

"Look, shoot me if you're gonna," Cody said, "but please, you have to call someone. My mom needs a doctor. She never did anything to you."

"You know, Cody, I'd really like to care," Lovell said. "But I'm afraid I don't."

That did it. Cody tore free of the toad and flung himself at Lovell. The toad swore, no idea where to aim as Cody and Lovell went sprawling across the sofa and rolled onto the floor. The big guy left his post at the door, grabbed Cody and peeled him off Lovell.

Cody flailed and struggled, but the big guy was a brick wall. The toad had finally settled on where to point his gun. At me. I returned the favor and we stood there, frozen and bristling, staring into each other's muzzles. Out of the corner of my eye I saw Lovell getting his unsteady feet under him. He was flushed a furious crimson and bleeding from the nose.

"Will somebody please shoot that fucking kid already," he said.

"Don't," I said to the toad, but I could see the big guy reaching for his gun. I knew the toad would blow me away the second I pointed my gun anywhere but at him. "Don't!" I repeated, like a dog barking. Just a desperate, angry sound with no real meaning.

Then I saw Hank moving towards them, fast and low. He kicked the big guy's knee, making it buckle sickeningly in the wrong direction. The guy bellowed like a branded bull, clutched his leg and collapsed, taking out the cheap coffee table as he went down. Hank had no problem taking the gun from him.

"Drop it," he said, drawing down on the toad.

Outnumbered now, the toad slowly lowered his gun. I took that opportunity to step up and stick the Sig in his ear.

"Let's have it," I told him, gesturing with an open hand for his gun.

"Fuck you," he said. "I ain't giving you shit, lady."

"Cody," Hank said, gun still trained on the toad. "Go on and call that ambulance for your momma."

Cody nodded and crossed the room to pick up the cordless phone.

"It's too late anyway," Lovell said.

"What?" Cody turned to Lovell, fists clenching.

"Just look at her," Lovell said. "She's dead. Overdosed. Bled out. Her forearm's cut open clear to the bone. Frankly, I'm amazed she didn't die sooner."

"Mom?" Cody dropped down on one knee beside his prone mother. "Mom?"

"Tragic, really."

"Vernon," Hank said. "You open your mouth again and it'll be my pleasure to shoot you dead. I've had all I'm gonna take from you."

"Mom!" Cody wailed.

"Way to go, Cody," Lovell said. "Takes a real man to get both his fucking parents killed."

True to his word, Hank shot Lovell in the face.

The toad spun, startled by the sound and I managed to knock the gun from his hand and then dance backward, out of his range. I raised the Sig and drew a bead on his forehead, freezing him halfway through a step. Lovell did a funny little backwards shuffle, waving arms outstretched like he was making fun of a blind person, then crumpled and hit the carpet beside the big guy.

"Hank," I said. "We need to get out of here, now."

"Get up," Hank said to the big guy.

"I can't, man," the guy replied. "My leg's busted."

For a moment, no one moved. Then several things happened at once. The big guy lunged for the toad's fallen pistol. The toad grabbed my gun hand, digging his left thumb into the soft underside of my wrist and forcing it downward while throwing a tight right at my face. I turned my head just enough to take it on the cheek instead of the nose and my vision went red. I heard a shot. Then another.

I staggered back, shaking my head. When my vision cleared, I was almost afraid to look.

But I did. The big guy was dead on his back, shot in the chest, the toad's gun in his hand. The toad was shot too, but not quite dead. He was face down in front of the recliner, hands still scrabbling weakly like independent creatures trying to get away. Hank stood over the big guy, gun in hand.

"You okay, Angel?" he asked.

I touched the throbbing spot on my cheekbone where the toad's knuckles had connected. I'd had worse.

"Fine," I said. "We'd better get rid of these bodies."

Hank nodded, running a shaking hand over his scalp.

"Get some blankets, shower curtains, whatever," I told him. "And help me get them into the back of the Suburban."

"Yeah," Hank replied. "But what about..."

He turned towards Cody, still hunched over his dead mother and talking softly to her, holding one of her limp hands.

"We leave her," I said.

"He's not gonna like that," Hank said.

"He doesn't have a choice," I said.

Hank ducked into another room. When he returned with a bundle of sheets under one arm he paused in the doorway, leaning against the frame. His hands were shaking harder now, eyes squeezed down to slits.

"Hank?" I asked, with an eyebrow raised.

"Come on," he said, pressing the heel of his free hand into his temple. "Let's get this over with."

He took a step towards Lovell's body, then staggered, flattening his palm against the wall to steady himself.

"God…" he swallowed the rest of the curse behind gritted teeth.

"What's wrong, Hank?"

"Just get Cody and I'll take care of this," Hank said.

I nodded and knelt beside Cody. He was still holding his mother's hand, shadow-eyed, not crying.

"Cody, we need to go now," I said.

No response.

Behind me, Hank dropped the sheets and started retching, vomiting against the wall. Cody looked up at the sound.

"Hank?"

Cody got to his feet and ran to Hank's side.

"Hank," Cody said. "Shit. Do you have your Imitrex?"

Hank wiped his mouth with his knuckles and nodded, pulling a prescription bottle from his pocket but he was unable to open it with his shaking hands.

"Here." Cody took the bottle and opened it, dumping a whole pharmacy of various candy-colored medication into his huge palm. "It's the little triangles, right?"

Hank tried to nod, but started retching again.

"Okay, okay," Cody said picking out the triangular pills. "Take these, but try not to throw up any more if you can help it. You really need to keep this down."

Cody got the pills into Hank's mouth and slung one of Hank's arms over his shoulder.

"Get Hank out to the truck," I said. "Quickly. I'll take care of this."

Choke Hold

Of course, that was easier said than done. The toad was finally dead, so I retrieved my Warthog and stuck it and the Sig in my go-bag. I managed to wrap all three bodies in the stained sheets, but getting them out to the Suburban was a different story. The toad was the smallest of the three, short and no more than twenty pounds heavier than me, but the dead weight was still a bitch to move. I ended up half carrying, half dragging him. Once I got him over by the back of the Suburban, I knew I wasn't gonna be able to get him up and in without help.

Cody was over on the passenger side of the truck, fussing over Hank. I whistled softly, waving him over.

"I need a hand here," I said.

He nodded and tossed the toad's body into the Suburban like it was laundry.

"You okay?" I asked.

He didn't answer, just shrugged.

"Look, here's what I need you to do," I told him. "First, help me get the other two bodies into the Suburban. Then I'll drive it, following you and Hank in his truck until we find a good place to ditch them. Got it?"

Still silent, he did what I asked. Moving the big guy nearly wiped us both out, but we managed. I got my go-bag, then climbed in behind the wheel. I was about to start the Suburban when Cody rapped his knuckles on the window. I rolled it down.

"I need a minute with her," he said. "Just one minute. To say goodbye."

I made myself take a deep breath before responding. No point snapping at a kid who's lost both his parents in the space of forty-eight hours. On the other hand, I wasn't so sympathetic that I was willing to wait around until the cops showed up just to make sure he got his emotional closure.

"One minute, Cody," I said. "Not one second more."

But he was already halfway to the door.

It was the longest minute of my life.

22.

I was about to go back in there and drag Cody out of the house when the kid reappeared in the doorway and ran to Hank's truck. As he fired up the noisy engine, I swore I could hear sirens in the distance. We got the hell out of there.

Despite Cody's warning about keeping the medication down, we still had to stop several times for Hank to stagger out onto the rocky shoulder and vomit. I was feeling keyed up and deeply paranoid, just waiting to be pulled over. We couldn't dump that damn Suburban soon enough.

Cody knew the area better than any of us and it wasn't long before he found a perfect spot, a hairpin turn on a winding mountain road. The guardrail had been hit more than once and was deeply crumpled, ready to snap. In the moonless night, the stunning landscape looked like some barren and hostile alien planet.

Cody left Hank in the truck and together he and I pushed the Suburban into the crumpled guardrail. The twisted metal tore like paper under the big vehicle's weight. It disappeared into the ravine like a stone slipping under still water, soundless for several seconds before it hit the rocks far below.

We stood together for a moment, not speaking, not looking at each other. It was a cool, clear night, like the night we met. Without a word, we turned and walked back to Hank's truck.

I sat in the middle of the bench seat, squeezed in between

the two men with my go-bag at my feet. To my right, Hank leaned against the window, still shirtless and using the replacement t-shirt Cody had given him to cover his eyes. His body was tense with obvious discomfort. To my left, Cody drove in stunned silence. I wanted to open him up, get him talking about what had happened, but when I tried, he shushed me, tipping his chin towards Hank. Cody told me in a whisper that even the low rumble of the truck's engine was excruciating for Hank while he was in the grip of one of his migraines. We needed to be as quiet as we could until the worst of the symptoms had passed.

So I didn't speak. I sat there, watching the winding road as the truck reluctantly climbed the 95 north, higher and higher into the mountains. The poor old truck was unhappy with our chosen route and made its opinion known by smoking and spluttering, releasing a desperate kind of burning metal smell into the cab. Just over an hour into the drive, the truck started shaking so hard that we had no choice but to pull over. Fortunately we were able to coast into a gas station just outside Quartzsite. Unfortunately, once Cody turned the engine off, it flat out refused to start again.

The garage was closed, but the tiny convenience store was still open. The Mexican woman behind the counter informed us that the garage wouldn't reopen until Monday, but that there was a motel down the road.

I could sense Cody going hot and tense, getting ready to flip out. I put my hand on his arm.

"Go get some water for Hank," I said, giving him a slight shove towards the cooler. "We don't want him to get dehydrated. I'll handle this."

Cody nodded and did as he was told. I turned back to the woman behind the counter.

"We need to be in Vegas by eight tomorrow morning," I said in the calmest, most even tone I could muster. "Is there somewhere we can rent a car?"

"Maybe over in Blythe," the woman said without taking her eyes off a small fuzzy television bolted to the ceiling, playing a Spanish *telenovela*. "But not before eight on a Sunday."

"Listen," I said, moving to block her view of the screen. "Isn't there some other option?"

She shrugged. "Sorry."

I briefly considered the Sig in my bag but I unzipped my money belt instead. I peeled off two twenties, setting them on the counter.

"Find someone who can come out and fix my truck right now, tonight, and I'll pay double what they normally charge."

She eyed the money, shrugged again. I added two more bills.

"I'll make some calls," she said, sweeping the bills off the counter and into a large purple purse. "But I can't promise nothing."

She took out a cellphone. After a few attempts, she launched into a rapid-fire Spanish conversation. The only thing I understood was *gringos locos*.

"Okay," she said. "My nephew will do it, but he can't promise for sure that it can be fixed without looking at it. Either way you gotta pay in advance. For the labor, you know. Overtime."

"How much," I said.

She pointed to my money belt. "The rest of what you got in there."

The Sig was looking like a better and better option.

Cody returned from the cooler with an armful of water bottles.

"Be reasonable," I said, still fighting to maintain civility.

"You don't wanna pay it, no problem," she said. "I can call Chuy right now and tell him to forget it."

"Angel, if we don't get moving again, and soon, we're fucked," Cody said, his voice tight and panicked. "What are we gonna do?"

"Don't worry, kid," I said. "Go give Hank the water. We'll be there in time."

"But…"

"Go on," I said.

"Hey," the woman said as he walked out. "He has to pay for that!"

"Let's call it part of the package," I said. I also selected a candy bar and a small packet of condoms to replace the one he broke. I wasn't about to let that sort of thing happen again.

Then I put the stack of bills on the counter. It was a lot—too much. But the truth was, I never kept all my money in one place and the amount in the belt was only about half of what I had on me. That didn't mean I liked giving it up—I needed every dollar I had—but I'd made the promise to get Cody to Vegas and god fucking dammit I was gonna do it.

Besides, I thought there was a better than even chance this bitch and her nephew were going to try to fuck us over, and if they did that, I'd happily take the money back by force, and carjack them too while I was at it. Asshole tax.

The nephew, Chuy, arrived then, buttoning up a stained coverall as he shouldered open the door of his truck. He was young and sullen, and looked like he'd been dragged out of bed, but not sleeping. He smelled like a porn set in August.

The woman spoke to him in Spanish and he replied. She handed him my money.

"Show him the truck," she said to me.

The nephew didn't speak much English at all, so the woman reluctantly came along to translate. After several minutes of poking around under the hood, he let us know, via his aunt, that he could fix it, but he needed a part. He was confident that he could "find" this part, implying that he was planning to steal it, but said he needed a few hours.

"Okay," I said. Then, to Cody: "We'll go check into that motel, let Hank lie down for a little while. As long as we get on the road by four, we won't have any problem getting you to Matt Kenner's place in time for the show."

The young mechanic looked up sharply when he heard the name Matt Kenner. He said something to the woman and she shrugged. She seemed to be very good at that.

"He wants to know if you like the fighter Matt Kenner," she said.

"Like him?" Cody said. "I'm on Team Kenner for the new season of *All American Fighter*."

The woman translated. Chuy cracked a huge smile and pumped Cody's hand like he was a presidential candidate.

Cody smiled back and then jerked his thumb towards Hank, who was still slumped in the passenger seat with his shirt over his eyes.

"That's Hank 'The Hammer' Hammond," Cody said. "He's my trainer."

Apparently that didn't need any translation. Chuy ran to the passenger door and tapped on the glass. Hank took the shirt off his eyes and looked up with a weak smile. He opened the door and got unsteadily to his feet. Chuy grabbed his hand with a flood of Spanish that the woman didn't even bother to try and translate.

"Hammer!" the mechanic said, struggling with the most rudimentary English. "Fight Japan very good. Number one!"

He fumbled in his many pockets and pulled out a pencil stub and a folded garage invoice, mimicking writing and then handing them to Hank.

"Sure thing," Hank said. "You bet."

He signed his name with a shaking hand. Chuy thanked him repeatedly in English and Spanish, took the autograph like it was a sacred relic and then turned around and handed me back my money.

"Free to Hammer," he said with a grin.

23.

We walked over to the motel the woman had pointed out. The Desert Rose. It was a flea pit, but had the advantage of being nearly empty. Less then half of the two dozen rooms seemed to be occupied. We got a room on the second floor, with a view of the gas station so I could keep an eye on our new best friend Chuy.

Hank took more pills and lay down on the bed with a damp washcloth over his eyes. Cody went out to investigate the snack machine but when he didn't come back after fifteen minutes, I left Hank dozing and went out to look for him.

I found him out on the breezeway, working his charms on a young, kittenish thing from one of the other rooms. Bleached hair cut into a trendy, uneven mop. Pouty pierced lip. Lots of smeary eyeliner. She was intricately tattooed, a little tipsy and obviously smitten, listening enraptured to his highly embellished story about drug dealers trying to kill him.

"Cody," I said. "A word?"

The girl retreated into her room, but made a big show of not closing the door all the way.

"Don't be jealous, baby," Cody said with a wink. "She means nothing to me." He looked across the street at Hank's truck and his face turned dark and serious. "Look, I need this. I'm going nuts here. I just need to…not think for a little while."

I understood, probably better than he would ever know.

"You don't mean anything to me either, kid," I said. "Not

like that, anyway. But I'd really rather you stay alive, okay? So by all means, have at it. But do me two favors. First of all, stay out of sight."

"Right," he said. "Sorry."

"And second, keep your mouth shut about what's happening. I'm serious. Don't tell anybody about what happened with Lovell. Not even semi-fictional variations on the story. Just tell 'em you're going to Vegas to be on *All American Fighter*. That should be more than enough to get you laid."

He nodded. "Fair enough."

"Go on, willya," I said, gesturing towards the girl's partially open door. "Go get her, Tiger."

Cody grinned.

"Cool," he said. "Don't wait up."

He swaggered off to his tryst looking so much like his father that I felt that little twisting hook inside my heart again. I wondered what was going to happen to that kid. Even if he made it to Vegas in one piece, even if he beat the odds, made it as a fighter and became a huge star, would he spiral inevitably down into addiction just like his father? Would he have what Hank had referred to as a "good corner," not just to help win in the ring but to help him navigate the corrupt fight game and avoid being taken by all the scumbags and users out there looking to eat ambitious little boys for breakfast?

I stood, looking out into the nearly empty parking lot and the dusty desert emptiness beyond. Thinking of the fight game and the adult film industry. Strange how similar they seemed. Young men fighting to become this ultimate over-the-top expression of manhood. Young female porn stars striving to become the ultimate expression of feminine allure. A few made it and became big stars, but most got chewed up and spat out, crippled by addiction, chronic pain and daddy issues before they hit thirty.

Daddy issues. Man, that's a big one. Some of us beat them and some of us didn't, but there's no question that most of us had them to one degree or another. Daddy doesn't love his little girl and she becomes a porn star. Or maybe he loves her too much, the wrong kind of love. If Daddy doesn't love his little boy, does the boy become a fighter? Obviously that wasn't true in every case—nothing is that simple—but the comparison felt painfully apt for me and Cody. I pictured ten-year-old Cody, lonely and rudderless, while Vic was off selling crystal meth to girls on the downside of the business. Then I thought of my own father, the utter contempt and disgust on his face as he stood there holding a videocassette in one hand, the other slowly closing into a fist.

We each seemed to have found a way to fill that Daddy-shaped hole, Cody by caring for his mother and playing nursemaid to Hank and his headaches, me with my girls, my agency.

I missed my girls. I missed all their silly drama and bad decisions. I missed being there to help them avoid the pitfalls of the adult industry and teaching them how to walk away with a decent nest egg. It had felt good to help people, something I hadn't had much opportunity to do on the run. I realized then that it wasn't just my promise to a dead man keeping me stubbornly stuck with Cody. It was lonely to have no one to look out for but myself.

I shook myself out of my reverie. Here I was, after warning him to stay out of sight, standing on the breezeway with a bullseye on my forehead. I turned around and headed back to our room.

When I pushed the door open, Hank was sitting up in bed, washcloth in one hand. He looked up when he heard me come in.

"How's the head?" I asked.

"Better," he replied. "Where's Cody?"

"He met a girl," I said. "I figure he'll be safe in her room for an hour or two."

"His momma ain't been dead six hours and that boy can still charm the panties off the Virgin Mary," Hank said. " 'Course, he'd have every right if he were a little bit relieved she's gone. You don't know how hard it's been on him, taking care of her all these years when she shoulda been taking care of him. Now this." He shrugged. "Guess I can't hardly blame the boy for wanting a little female distraction."

"What about you, Hank?" I asked. "What do you do for female distraction? You got a girlfriend?"

He grinned, shaking his stone idol head.

"Nah," he said. "Too ugly, I reckon."

"Come on now," I said. "You can't tell me you don't get all kinds of offers from those lonely MILFs that bring their kids in to your grappling classes."

He shrugged, looking around for some place to put down the wet washcloth. There wasn't anywhere, so he just held on to it.

"Not really," he said. "I mean, I ain't got time for that kind of thing, what with training and teaching and all." He looked down at the washcloth. "How about you? You got somebody special?"

"Me?" I smiled. "I don't have time for that kind of thing either, what with trying to avoid getting killed and all."

He laughed, then turned quickly serious.

"What happened to you, Angel?" he asked.

I wanted to tell him everything, but I had no idea where to begin. I'd spent so much time trying to forget that it all seemed foreign to me now, like the plot of a movie I'd heard described but never seen.

"Some men hurt me," I said eventually. "I hurt them back."

"So you said," Hank replied. "A vigilante."

"Right," I said. More silence, and then: "But there was this one guy…"

I turned and walked over to the window, peering through the curtains at the gas station. I could see Hank's truck, but not Chuy. He must have been off trying to "find" the part.

"I should have killed him," I said. "But I didn't. At the time, he seemed like a small part of the big picture, and so I left him in the hands of others. They decided to let him live. It was stupid of me, I know that now. Too late of course. He was deported as soon as he had healed enough to fly. I hoped I'd never see him again."

"And now you find yourself on the other end of the vendetta?"

"Maybe," I said. "Or maybe he's just doing his job, hunting me down on behalf of the boss I testified against. Doesn't really matter which."

Neither of us said anything for about a year. Hank twisted the washcloth back and forth in his fists. I didn't want to talk about the past anymore, so I came forward and sat down on the bed beside him. I took the washcloth out of his hands, letting it drop to the floor.

He turned to me but couldn't hold my gaze for more than a second. His big shoulders were hunched and tense. I kissed him.

At first he was stiff and frozen against me as I tried to open his mouth with my tongue, moving my hands across the hard, tectonic plates of his muscular back. Then, without warning, he lunged into the kiss with a sudden, violent ferocity so intense that it scared me a little and made me wonder if maybe I'd made a terrible mistake. But that kind of crazy animal lust is contagious and pretty soon I was beyond wondering about anything at all. This was what I had wanted all along.

I could just cut to the blowing curtains at this point and let you fill in the blanks, but this wasn't a scene out of some romantic chickflick. Real life isn't always so pretty and perfect and the truth couldn't have been farther from my fantasy of what it might be like with him.

He couldn't stay hard.

When it finally became obvious that despite all my clever professional tricks, it just wasn't gonna happen, he pushed away and sat on the edge of the bed with his head in his hands.

"Hey," I said softly, reaching out to touch his shoulder.

He shook off my hand and stood. He pulled on his jeans and left the room, shoeless and bare-chested.

When a half hour had passed and he still hadn't come back, I wrapped the sheet around myself and stuck my head out the door.

He was standing three doors down, squinting at the room

number and pounding his fist against his temple. His face was blotchy and damp like he'd been crying.

"Hank," I said softly.

He jumped at the sound of my voice.

"I…" He looked back at the door of the room he was standing in front of. "I forgot the room number."

"Please," I said. "Come back inside."

He did, and I double locked the door behind him. I peered out through the curtains at the empty breezeway, then walked back over to the bed and pulled the covers over my legs.

After a while, he came slowly over and sat on the edge of the bed, facing away.

"I'm sorry about before," he said.

"Don't be," I told him.

I was about to tell him it was nothing, but he cut me off.

"It's been like this for about seven years now," he said. "It was on and off at first but ever since…well it just kept getting worse and worse. I'm fine when I'm alone, but I can't…It's like I start to panic and then I think…I don't know. I just can't. I used to keep on trying, thinking it'd be different with the right woman. But…well, eventually I just gave up."

I didn't say anything.

"It's like…" He hung his head. "You're so pretty and I get scared…I don't want to hurt you."

I kept my mouth shut and put my hand on his shoulder again. This time he didn't shake it off. I could see goosebumps flare up across his back.

"You're not mad?" he asked.

"Of course not."

"Normally, women seem to get pretty annoyed about it,"

he said. "Sometimes they'll tell me it doesn't matter, but then they suddenly get real busy and stop returning my calls."

"I'm hardly what you'd call normal," I said.

"That makes two of us," he said. Then: "Can I ask a favor?" Almost too soft to hear.

"Sure," I replied.

"This is gonna sound stupid," he said. He still wouldn't turn around to face me.

"Go ahead," I said.

"If you don't mind," he said. "Could you just…well, I swear I can't remember the last time somebody had their arms around me for more than ten seconds and wasn't trying to break my wrist or punch me in the face. You don't have to do nothing else, I just…I want to remember what that feels like."

"How do you know I won't try to punch you in the face?" I asked.

He laughed all in a rush, like he'd been holding his breath.

"Well," he said, finally turning to look at me. "I guess that's just a chance I'll have to take."

I pulled him close to me and lay back so that we were side by side. He closed his eyes and leaned his head against my neck. I'm not much of a cuddler, but I did my best for him, figuring it was the least I could do after everything we'd been through together. I ran my palm up over his prickly scalp and down the back of his neck and he made a soft little noise like a hurt dog. He was holding on to me so tightly I could hardly breathe and I was intensely aware of every point of contact between us. I never did get off during our failed attempt and was still painfully turned on, feeling like I might go crazy from being so close to something I couldn't have.

And, to tell the truth, all that raw, powerful emotion pouring off him like sweat was scaring the shit out of me. I needed to grab the reins, to take control before things got totally out of hand, but I couldn't. Sex just wasn't an option and I was utterly out of my element.

I noticed he was no longer afraid of eye contact. And now that he was really looking at me, I could see I was in trouble. I could see that he was falling. Hard.

"Angel," he was saying against my neck. "That's just what you are. An angel."

His breath was hot on my skin, his thick fingers combing awkwardly through my hair. I was starting to feel anxious and uncomfortable.

"Look, I know I ain't no kinda prize," he said. "Broke down, used up, no good in the sack and can't even think straight half the time. But…" He looked up at me again, eyes clear and pale as rain. "If you'll have me, Angel, well…then maybe I ain't a lost cause after all."

"Hank…" I started, but trailed off.

Now I was the one who couldn't make eye contact. I had no idea what I was supposed to say. Sex is my superpower, but when it comes to real intimacy, I'm like a clueless teenager. This had gone way too far, way too fast, and I was in way over my head.

I was almost relieved when armed men kicked in the door.

24.

Two guys, similar as brothers. Conservative dark hair, aquiline profiles and silenced handguns. Both wore gold chains and track suits, one white and one navy blue. When White Track Suit spoke up, his heavy Croatian accent confirmed what I already knew in my nauseous, twisting gut.

"Get up, Angel," he said. "Put on clothes, please."

Navy Track Suit closed the door behind him, or as closed as it could get with its now splintered frame and twisted lock. The two of them stepped into the room, standing between the door and the small alcove that led to the bathroom. White Track Suit used his gun to gesture to my fallen bra, in case I may not have understood.

I moved to the foot of the bed and got slowly to my feet, reaching for my scattered clothing without taking my eyes off the two men. Behind me, Hank was pulling on his shirt on the other side of the bed, tense and bristling. My go-bag was on the table against the wall, just out of reach. A desperate tightness was closing down my throat, making it hard to breathe.

I had gotten into my shorts, bra and shoes and was hunting for my tank top when I saw Hank lunge forward out of the corner of my eye. He grabbed the edge of the mattress and flipped it up, using it to shove the Croatians backward into the little alcove by the bathroom.

"Go!" he shouted, but didn't need to. I had the go-bag over my shoulder and was already halfway out.

The Croatians began shooting through the mattress. Hank let go and leaped back. I pulled out the Sig and motioned for Hank to make a break for the door. As he did I put a few rounds into the mattress, causing the Croatians behind it to dive into the bathroom. I followed Hank out the door.

Out on the breezeway, Hank gave the doublewide snack machine beside our door a heroic shove, veins standing out in his forehead. The machine slid, blocking the door to our room.

"Where's Cody?" Hank asked.

I pointed to the door of the girl's room. "Maybe we should…"

I was about to say maybe we should leave him there, lead the Croatians away from him to keep him safe, when a chair came crashing through the window to our room. The Croatians would be out on the breezeway in a heartbeat. Even running, there was no time to make it to the staircase at the far left, and the now broken window of our room was between us and the center stairway. I grabbed the doorknob of the girl's room, hoping Cody had been too horny to remember to lock the door. Lucky for us, he had.

Cody had the girl on her back on the bed, clutching one of her slender legs to his chest and trying to stuff all five of her pink leopard painted toes into his mouth while nailing her into next week.

When we burst in, he let out a surprised grunt, muffled by toes. The girl squealed and rolled away, covering her cute little tits with her tattooed arms. When she saw the gun in my hand, she screamed. Hank grabbed her and put a hand over her mouth while I shut the door.

"What the…?" Cody asked, making no attempt to cover himself.

I hissed at him to be quiet, finger pressed to my lips.

Cody was smart and shut up quick, his eyes wide as swift shadows passed on the other side of the cheap curtains. Shouting echoed in the stairwell.

Then, nothing.

"Get dressed, willya?" I whispered. "Before you put someone's eye out." Then to the girl: "You too, honey. Got a car? We need to get the hell out of here."

Hank took his hand off the girl's mouth.

"Codeeeeeee," she wailed.

"It's okay, Madison," he said. "Keep your voice down. We aren't gonna let anything happen to you. Just get dressed."

"Do you have a car?" I asked again. "Or don't you."

" 'Course I do," the girl stage-whispered, wiggling back into her tiny jean shorts and halter top and grabbing a huge zebra-striped hobo purse festooned with jangling chains.

Hank stepped over to the door and listened, then cautiously pulled it open. Nobody shot him so I figured it was safe. Together, the four of us moved in a tight little knot out onto the breezeway. I could hear footsteps in the stairwell on the far end, but I couldn't tell if they were going up or down. Staying close to the wall, we walked quickly around the corner to the center stairs. It looked clear at the bottom. I went down first, then Cody and Madison. Hank took the rear.

Those center steps seemed to be primarily for use by maids and led not to the front of the building but around the back where the laundry machines and housekeeping supplies were kept. To the right of the landing was the back door to the office, propped open with a forty-ounce beer bottle. I opened the door and slipped inside, motioning for the others to follow.

The dimly lit back room of the office area had been set up as a sort of personal living quarters. The front, public area was visible through a beaded doorway. A shabby velveteen sofa with a crumpled blanket stood in for a bed. Flickering television. Dorm refrigerator. Scarred coffee table with a surprisingly high-end laptop sitting open and positioned to be reachable from the sofa. Its screen whirled with random swooshes of color.

When Cody and Madison came into the room, one of them must have bumped against the low coffee table because the screensaver on the laptop disappeared, revealing an open browser. In the center of the lurid pink webpage was a large surveillance photo of me with Cody on one side and Hank on the other.

I bent down for a closer look. The website on display was something called PornSighted.com and featured candid cell-phone photos of porn stars in the laundromat, grocery store or Starbucks. My photo was labeled "Double Dare?" Under it, a breathless caption:

chick that looks just like angel dare just checked into the motel where i work, rented 1 room with 2 guys! have a bet going - need a ruling, dare or not?

The name, address and phone number of the motel were automatically stamped on the bottom right of the image, along with the date and time.

I was ready to kill the clerk, but it turned out the Croatians had beat me to it. Looked like they were pretty enthusiastic about it too, but I didn't feel that bad for the bastard. He should have minded his own damn business.

I thought Madison was gonna go all screamy again when she saw the clerk's body on the office floor, but she didn't. She just clung tighter to Cody as they inched around the edges of the spreading stain, her eyes wide.

I peered out between the blinds. No sign of the track suits, but there was a third guy standing beside the open door of a Japanese import, smoking a cigarette. He was a little younger and not as attractive as his two friends. Dirty blond with a wide, moony face and a sullen expression, he gave off a distinct little-brother-made-to-wait-in-the-car vibe. He was craning his neck to look up at the second-floor breezeway like he was hoping to catch a glimpse of the action he was missing. The car was running.

"Madison," I said. "Which car is yours?"

"It's the black Nova there on the end," she said.

"Fine," I said. "Keys."

The girl started digging through her huge purse.

I looked out again, saw the Nova. Good news, it was on the end of the lot closest to us. Bad news, the little brother was between us and it.

"Hurry up," I said over my shoulder.

"I'm looking," she said. "I can't find anything in this damn purse."

She turned the purse upside down, dumping its contents on the carpet. Makeup. Tampons. Cellphone. Crumpled receipts. Sparkly purple wallet. Giant white plastic sunglasses. Change. Pills. Candy. No keys.

"Shit," Cody said. "Remember we were using that little pink vibrator?"

"Dammit!" Madison said. "You're right."

"What the hell does that have to do with keys?" I asked.

"The vibrator," Madison said. "It's on my keychain."

"The keys must still be on the nightstand." Cody said. "I'll go back up and get them."

"No," I said. "Bad idea. We need to stay together."

"Y'all just get ready to run," Hank said, easing the door open. "Watch for my signal."

Then he was gone.

I looked out through the blinds but couldn't see him anywhere. It was like he'd disappeared the second he passed through the door. I watched the little brother with a slippery knot in my belly, waiting.

A minute passed, then another. Nothing happened. Then the little brother fell forward with a surprised expression and a breathless whoosh, disappearing between two cars. No one started shooting and seconds later, Hank stood up in the little brother's place, motioning for us to come out.

"Get in the back seat," I said to Cody. "Keep her close and go as quickly as you can."

The two made the dash for the car. I sucked in a big breath and followed.

Once I was out the door, I spun and aimed the Sig up at the breezeway, scanning for signs of movement. Nothing at first, but then just when I was about halfway to the car, the door to Madison's room opened and White Track Suit stepped out.

I squeezed off a shot in his direction, aiming for the doorframe and hoping to scare him into ducking back into the room. His shiny white track pants blossomed red just above the left knee and he let out a furious string of Croatian profanity. I sprinted for the car. Navy Track Suit had come out shooting at that point, tossing up puffs of grit and sand all around me.

Hank was behind the wheel by the time I dove into the passenger seat. He reversed out of the lot and floored it. The car took a few hits to the body, but the tires were unscathed. I guess I got lucky when I took out White Track Suit. He was obviously the better shot of the two.

We left the motel in the rearview mirror.

"You okay to drive?" I asked Hank.

"Reckon I'll be all right for a little while," he said. "So long as we don't run into no cops. Then again, if we do run into the law, me driving without a license is the least of our sins."

"Who the hell were those guys, Angel?" Cody asked.

"Those guys are my problem," I replied.

"Bullshit," Cody said, sitting forward and putting a hand on the back of my seat. "They saw all of us together. Whoever they are, they're *our* problem now. We have a right to know."

"Fair enough," I said, but then didn't know how to continue.

I looked out the window at a lot of black desert nothing then down at my hands.

"Okay, look, it's like this," I said. "Couple years ago, I testified against a very bad man. A man who was importing Eastern European women to the States for use as sex slaves. That man went down for what he did, but he has friends."

"Whoa!" Madison said. "Angel…? You're Angel Dare! Holy

shit, I can't believe I didn't recognize you right away. You're my hero! You're like…like the Crow of porn."

I tried not to laugh, but couldn't help it. I wondered if she'd seen *Phoenix Rising*.

"Y'all want to tell me where we're going?" Hank asked.

"Madison?" I asked. "Is there somewhere we can drop you off, somewhere safe?"

"Can you give me a lift to Havasu City?" she asked. "I'm booked to dance the afternoon shift tomorrow at Peachy's and I've got an aunt there I can stay with until I get things sorted out. Just get on the 95 north and when we get closer, I'll tell you which way to go, okay?"

A stripper. Why didn't that surprise me?

"You bet," Hank said.

He reached across the seat, took my hand and brought it to his lips, flashing that big boyish grin like there wasn't a thing wrong in the world. Like we'd won. I tried to smile back, but the effort was weak and hopeless. I knew the guys who were after me weren't gonna give up that easily. I took my hand back and started cleaning and reloading the Sig.

25.

We dropped Madison in front of a pink southwest-style home on the dramatically named Thundercloud Drive in Lake Havasu City. Cody walked her to the door and there was an interval of earnest necking, whispered promises and exchanging of phone numbers before the door was opened by a sleepy woman in a fuzzy white bathrobe. The woman ushered Madison inside with a resigned expression that made it clear this sort of thing happened all the time. Cody offered to drive and Hank was happy to let him.

"You want to lie down in the back seat, Angel?" Hank asked.

I did. But even as tired as I was I still couldn't find sleep. Hank and Cody were talking softly about the show, about Matt Kenner and the fight game in general. They might as well have been speaking Croatian.

I had finally drifted off when we arrived in Vegas. The neon woke me up. No matter how many times I'd been to Vegas, it always seemed so improbable. All that glitter and flash, yet perpetually unfinished and overrun with cranes. Like nothing could ever be big enough. It was barely 3 AM.

"We should check in somewhere," I said, rubbing my eye. "Try to grab a little sleep before we head over to Kenner's."

"I want to get there early," Cody said. "Seven at the latest."

"No problem," I said. "We'll set an alarm."

Cody pulled into the parking structure for the Four Queens. He wanted to get his own room, but I felt it would be safer to stay together. I won by agreeing to a suite with a separate bedroom. I was glad the starstruck mechanic had given me my money back.

Once we dragged ourselves up to the suite, Hank headed into the bathroom. Cody stood by the sink outside the bathroom door, splashing water on his face and looking into the mirror. His unshaven face was very pale, eyes deeply shadowed. I walked over, unwrapped a glass and filled it from the tap.

"You okay?" I asked, after downing the water.

"My mom must have tried to kill herself a dozen times since I was old enough to count," Cody said. "Maybe more. And every time they would pump her stomach or stitch up her wrists, part of me would be glad she was okay, but another part…" He looked up at his reflection, then at me. "I just want to have my own life. Does that make me a bad person?"

I didn't have an answer for him. I set the glass down on the counter.

"What are you gonna do after you drop me at Kenner's?" he asked.

I didn't have an answer for that one either.

"Are you scared?" he asked.

That was a no-brainer.

"Yes," I replied.

"Me too," he said.

He tried to pull me in for another one of his hugs.

"Knock it off, kid," I said with a smile. "Haven't you had enough for one day?"

"Nope," he said, reaching playfully for me again. "Come on, there's plenty to go around."

I swatted his big hands away and rolled my eyes.

"Jesus," I said. "Don't make me shoot you."

"I'm just playing," he said. He smiled, tipping his head towards the closed bathroom door. "You like him, huh?"

I frowned. "Hank? Sure, why?"

"I mean, you know… You're into him."

"What?" I turned away. Where the hell had that come from? "Of course not."

"It's cool," Cody said with a cocky shrug, like I could deny it all I wanted but he knew the real score.

He reached out and put an arm around me, leaning his cheek against the top of my head.

Hank came out of the bathroom. He froze for a moment in the doorway, backlit so I couldn't see his expression.

"Get your fucking hands off her," he said.

I was so flabbergasted by Hank's sudden profanity that I had no idea how to respond. The next thing I knew he'd grabbed Cody and hauled him off me.

He had a fistful of Cody's shirt twisted up under his chin and the other hand was cocked back, ready to let him have it.

"Hank," Cody said, his own hands up but open. "Hank, listen to me. You're not thinking right again."

"The hell I ain't," Hank said.

He swung that fist at Cody. Cody wrenched himself out of range, leaving behind a torn handful of shirt.

"Hank, stop it," I said, backing away. "This is nuts."

Hank stepped in with another swing, this one clipping Cody on the jaw as he danced backwards and sideways. Cody grabbed the desk chair and shoved it between him and Hank.

"Jesus," Cody said, hands still open, placating. "Would you just fucking…"

Hank threw the chair out of his way with such force that it lost a leg when it slammed into the far wall. Cody's head turned involuntarily towards the noise of the chair's demise and Hank let him have it hard.

That one was right on the money. Cody's head snapped back and he staggered, dropping to one knee.

"Motherfucker!" Cody spat, all patience gone now, temper boiling over as his hands coiled into fists.

He lunged at Hank. The two of them went down rolling, trading wild punches and knees to the body. I wanted desperately to do something to stop them, but felt utterly powerless in the wake of this testosterone-fueled madness. Until Hank grabbed that broken-off chair leg. At that point, I felt like I had no choice.

He was straddling Cody on the ground, holding the leg high while Cody cowered below, covering his face with his hands. I dove in and grabbed Hank's wrist.

"Look at me, Hank," I said, face inches from his and fighting for eye contact. I knew I didn't have a hope in hell of overpowering him or restraining him physically. I had to find another way to stop this. "Come on, now, look at me. You don't want to hurt Cody, do you?"

Hank finally turned to me but it seemed to take a second for him to really see me. Then he looked back down at Cody, made a wordless sound of anguish and dropped the chair leg. Cody squirmed out from under him, flushed bright red and bleeding from a cut above his left eye. Hank slammed his fist into his own temple.

"Fuck!" Cody said, touching the cut and wincing. "Go take your crazy pills, you fucking nutjob."

"Cody, please," I said. "Give me a minute."

Cody looked down and nodded, his face a warzone of conflicting emotions. He got his feet under him and retreated silently into the bedroom. Hank stood, his back to me.

"Hank," I said as softly as I could manage.

"I'm sorry," Hank said. "I don't know what got into me." He paused. Looked at me, then away again. "That's a lie," he said. "Truth is, I know exactly what's wrong with me, I just don't like to think about it."

He sat on the couch, elbows on his knees. I stood, waiting for him to continue.

"Doc's got a fancy name for it," he said. "But it's simple, really. I'm getting punchy." He tapped his temple with his scarred knuckles. "Knocked my brain around so many times that it don't work right no more. Sure, we've all seen it before with older fighters, joked about it even, but I never really believed it would happen to me."

I came over and sat beside him.

"Dizzy, headaches, can't remember nothing from one minute to the next." He pulled the pill bottle from his pocket and took a couple. "I get panic attacks, do these crazy, impulsive things and then I get to feeling so low, it's like I don't want to live." He looked up at me. "Do you know, before I met you, I was planning… Well I figured once Cody got with Team Kenner, I'd just quietly check out. Get it over with before I can't remember my name no more. Now, all of a sudden things are different."

He leaned into me and we lay down together on the

couch, silent for a minute. His big head was heavy as an anvil on my chest. I'd participated in more non-sexual cuddling during the past six hours than in the whole rest of my life. I felt like a fumbling virgin, imitating something I'd heard other girls talk about but never done myself.

"With you in my corner, Angel," he said, "I feel like I can keep on fighting it. I feel like…like maybe I could start over. Figure out how to be a decent man again. The kind of man you deserve."

What the hell was I supposed to say? I couldn't handle that kind of talk on top of everything else that had happened. I was so tired I was near delirious and the last thing in the world I needed was to get myself entangled in a serious relationship with a troubled man like Hank. All I wanted was to deliver Cody safely to Matt Kenner. I figured after that happened I would find a way to let Hank down as gently as I could.

"We'd better try and get a little sleep," I said.

"You're right," he said with a heavy sigh.

I don't think either of us really slept. Eventually an alarm went off in the other room and it was time to take Cody to Kenner's.

26.

Kenner's dojo was in a little industrial pocket off the strip, behind the Rio. When we arrived, an hour and fifteen minutes early, there was a young woman unlocking a security gate. I asked the cab driver to wait while the woman informed Cody in a nasal monotone that the shooting location for *All American Fighter: The Next Generation* had been moved to the Sands so they would have more space.

"Good thing we came early!" Cody said, trying for upbeat, but looking very pale and anxious. It had all been building up to this.

The cab dropped us in front of the Sands. Cody spotted a sign with the AAFC logo, the words TEAM KENNER and a big arrow. He immediately took off in that direction, pulling Hank and me along in his excited wake. His nervous energy was infectious.

After several wrong turns, we eventually found the conference room we were looking for. Cody was way ahead of me, so I couldn't see his face when we walked in, but I didn't need to. His body language said it all.

It was a cattle call. The room was enormous and filled with hundreds and hundreds of young men exactly like Cody, all hopeful faces and fight shorts and badly designed t-shirts. Half of them clutching business cards like the one Kenner had given Cody. Kenner himself was nowhere to be seen.

Hank and I hung back in the large double doorway while

Cody went from one brusque headset-wearing person to another, demanding to see Kenner. He was given several more or less profanity-laden versions of "Get in line, kid."

"Just calm down and think for a second," Hank told Cody when we caught up to him. "This ain't the end of the world. So it's an audition—you still got a decent shot here, better than most, I'd say. Don't blow what chance you got by…"

"No," Cody said. "No, this is bullshit." He started pacing frantically. "Bullshit. This is total fucking bullshit. I just need to talk to Kenner."

"Cody, listen to me now," Hank said.

"You don't know what he said to me." Cody stopped pacing and turned to Hank. "He said I was the best. The best he'd ever seen. I'm not waiting in line with all these douchebags. All I have to do is talk to Kenner and he'll take care of this bullshit. Kenner said…"

One of the other kids on the line leaned in and spoke out of the corner of his mouth.

"Kenner said he'd marry you after he fucked you? What a coincidence, that's what he told me, too!"

Other boys in the line started to snicker and Cody lunged at the sarcastic kid. Hank caught Cody and dragged him back just as a hulking security guard in a nylon jacket started making his way towards us.

"Is there a problem?" the guard asked.

"No sir," Hank replied. "No problem." He slowly loosened his grip on Cody, then let him go. "Ain't that right?"

"Right," Cody said, turning away, shoulders sagging. I could see the frustration in his eyes, the pain. But he bit it back. "No problem," he told the guard.

The guard walked back over the steps leading up to the large caged ring a group of staffers in *All American Fighter* crew t-shirts were setting up.

For a few minutes, nothing happened. The boys in the line talked and jostled each other. Tools clanged as the cage was assembled. There was a crackle of walkie-talkie static. Cody stood apart from us, silent and looking down at his shoes.

Then out of the crowd of boys, Madison. She turned every head in the room, but not because of her tiny shorts. It was her face.

I knew that face too well. Black eyes. Swollen, split lip, her cute little lip ring torn out. She was crying, running to Cody and throwing herself sobbing into his arms.

"I'm so sorry, Cody," she said. "I didn't want to tell them where you were, but they made me. You need to get out of here!"

Cody was losing it. I could see that. He had held it all together, sucked it up and kept going because his big chance was waiting on the other end. Now it was all falling apart.

"Stay with him," I told Hank, taking Madison by the arm and guiding her to the door.

"Listen to me," I said to her. "Things are going bad here, and I want you as far away from us as possible when that happens. Go find casino security and have them call the cops. Don't go anywhere alone until the cops get here. Not even to the bathroom, do you hear me?"

"Cody?" she called over my shoulder. He wouldn't turn to her voice.

"Go now," I said. "Hurry."

She looked up at me, eyes bruised and wet with tears.

"Tell him I'm sorry," she said. "I tried not to tell them."

It killed me to hear her say that. I wanted to sweep her up in my arms and tell her I understood so well it hurt, but there was no time.

"Go," I said again.

She ran.

I went back to where Hank was trying to talk Cody down. Cody had that thundery look, like he was gonna start throwing shit.

"We need to leave," I said. "Now."

"I'm not leaving," Cody said. "Not till I have a chance to talk to Kenner."

That's when Navy Track Suit and his sulky little brother showed up on the far side of the room, chatting up one of the headset girls. The little brother looked over and saw me. He made his forefinger and thumb into the shape of a gun and pointed at me, then winked.

"Now, Cody," I said.

No more argument from him. The three of us backed together out the door, turned towards the casino floor and walked right past the bleached-blond teenage killer who'd tried to run us off the road outside Duncan's Diner.

27.

"That's the guy," Cody said to Hank once we'd swiftly put some distance between us. "Holy shit, that's him! The guy from the diner!"

The blond kid was standing by an ATM talking on a cellphone, bookended by a pair of new teenage *compadres* to replace the ones that had been killed.

"But Lovell's dead," Cody said. "He couldn't have sent these guys."

"Lovell may have been a lying S.O.B.," Hank said, "but maybe he was telling the truth about not having a hand in that business."

"So who...?" Cody began.

"We can think about that later," I said as the blond kid glanced over in our direction. The look of surprise when he spotted us would have been funnier if I didn't know that he was here to finish the job he'd fucked up before. "Right now we just need to get the hell out of here."

The blond kid was standing between us and the main entrance. We couldn't go back the way we came because the Croatians had come out of the conference room behind us and were turning their heads back and forth like bloodhounds casting for a scent. I looked around, too, and spotted a large banner featuring a surgically enhanced platinum blonde whose candy pink lips matched her tiny bikini.

Beneath her in lurid pink letters: AVN ADULT ENTERTAINMENT EXPO.

"This way," I said.

We walked as fast as we could without looking like we were running, working our way through the clattering, jangling guts of the Sands and into the gigantic adjacent convention center. There was already a huge line waiting to get in. Mostly men. As I passed, a wash of excited whispers spread through the line. Austin, my former WitSec marshal, would have had a heart attack if he'd seen me here. Talk about contact with people from my former life.

AVN stands for *Adult Video News*. It's basically the porno *Variety*. The AVN Expo is the largest American event in the industry. You could also call it a gathering of the 30,000 people most likely to recognize Angel Dare.

I grabbed Cody and Hank and pulled them over to a large doorway labeled TRADE ENTRANCE.

"Name?" the bored-looking girl behind the welcome table said. Just my luck that she was the one out of 30,000 that had no idea who I was.

"Angel Dare," I said, looking back over my shoulder. The men who wanted us dead couldn't be far behind. It was just a question of which set would arrive first—and whether we could get past this woman before then.

She chewed her large, fruity wad of gum as she scanned the list on her clipboard. I felt panic building beneath my sternum. I could see the Croatians now, coming across the crowded lobby, working their way towards the entrance. I hadn't spotted the Mexican kid and his buddies yet, but that didn't mean they weren't here.

"I'm not seeing that name," she said. "Who are you with?"

"She's with me," said a deep, honeyed baritone as hands wrapped around my waist from behind.

I turned to a face I hadn't seen in ages. Larry Lynsky, also known as Marco Pole. The man I did my first scene with. His *Brand Spankin' New* series was one of the longest running and most popular amateur lines of all time. When we did our scene, he was in his late thirties and looked like a tattooed Errol Flynn. Now he'd packed on at least seventy-five pounds and lost most of his hair, but he still wore his trademark fedora and his eyes still had the same Mad Hatter sparkle. Beside me, I could feel Hank tensing up. I really hoped he wouldn't blow it with another violent burst of irrational jealousy.

"Marco," I said. "It's great to see you."

"Angel, dollface," he said. "You can't imagine the things I've heard."

"I'll bet I can," I said.

"Well you'd better fill me in," Marco said as he took my arm, patting my hand and leading me past the flummoxed girl with the clipboard.

"She can't go in if she's not on the list," the girl whined.

"Miss Desmond can!" Marco said with a flourish, dismissing her with a wave of his fat, ring-covered fingers and leading me through the doorway to the expo floor.

"I thought you said Dare," she called after us.

"That's not nice, Marco," I said. "I'm hardly the Norma Desmond of porn."

"Of course not, dear," he said. "But none of these bubble-headed young things appreciate my *Sunset Boulevard* references like you do."

I turned back and saw that the Croatians had just arrived at the desk. They were pointing in my direction and, god bless her, the gum-snapping gatekeeper was stonewalling them. She pointed to the long snaking line in front of the public entrance and a pair of large men in security jackets stepped up to make sure there was no trouble. The Croatians backed away, smiling and showing their palms. With luck, they'd be stuck waiting on line long enough for us to find another way out. Of course, once we got out of the convention center we'd be facing a bigger problem: getting out of Vegas.

"Tell me," Marco said. "Who are your friends?"

"This is Cody…" I paused. "Cody Ventura."

Marco raised his eyebrows and dropped his gaze to Cody's package.

"Thick Vic's kid?" he asked.

"Yeah," I said.

"Take after your father, do you?" Marco asked Cody.

"I got a big dick if that's what you're asking," Cody said, annoyed, still reeling from the AAFC letdown. But annoyance wasn't the only emotion he was displaying—I saw his head involuntarily swiveling to follow all the g-string-clad, high-heeled starlets walking the aisles.

"I'm running a live fan-fucker cam," Marco said. He winked at me. "Don't tell security." Then back to Cody: "You up for a quick scene, kid?"

"Scene?" Cody said.

"You want to fuck a pretty girl?"

I could see from the expression on his face that, having been whipsawed all morning, he'd finally been asked something he could answer definitively and with confidence. "Yeah," he said.

"On camera, you understand," Marco said.

Cody looked at me, almost like he was asking permission.

"Right now," I said, "being on a live webcam might be one of the safest places you could be."

"You okay with interracial?" Marco asked. "I got this gorgeous black girl, looks like a supermodel and fucks like the Tasmanian Devil."

"Sure," Cody said. "Why? Are there some guys that won't do it with black girls?"

"Crazy, huh?" Marco said. "The way I see it pussy's pussy, be it black, white, yellow or green. How about you, handsome?" Marco asked Hank. "Wanna join in for a DP?"

I had to smile at Hank's shocked expression.

"Just Cody," I told Marco.

Marco nodded. "No problem."

Looking over at Hank, I could see he'd interpreted what I'd done as a demonstration of loyalty and that instantly made me wish I'd kept my mouth shut. The longer I let this go on, the harder it was going to be to break it off. Of course, that depended on my living long enough to break anybody's heart, which right now didn't seem too likely.

We walked with Marco over to the PoleHer Productions booth. There were two girls sitting behind the table. One tall, black and lithe, the other a buxom redhead.

"Girls," Marco said. "I brought you a present."

The girls stood and came around the table to coo over Cody.

"Cherise St. Croix, Sunny Dee, this is Cody Ventura."

The black girl, Cherise, put her hand on Cody's action and purred.

"Mmmmmmm," she said. "Nice."

"How old are you, honey?" Sunny asked.

"Eighteen," Cody replied, eyes riveted on the big dark nipples poking up through Cherise's flimsy lacy top.

"License," Sunny said, holding out her sparkle-nailed hand.

Cody shot an anxious look back at me. I nodded and he dug out his wallet, handing over his driver's license. Sunny pulled out a large, professional quality camera, laid Cody's license out on the table and shot several photos.

"Come on, baby," Cherise said, placing that familiar blue diamond-shaped Vitamin V on Cody's tongue. "I'll take good care of you."

She kissed him and then led him off into an enclosed private area behind the booth.

"So my dearest," Marco said, "where have you been keeping your gorgeousness?"

"Marco," I said. "You know I love you, but now is not the time for catch-up."

"What is it?" Marco said. "What kind of trouble are you in, beautiful?"

"The kind you don't need," I said.

The last thing I wanted was to get him involved in this mess. I'd brought too much pain to too many of my friends by involving them in my troubles.

Looking down the line of booths, past a fucking machine and a display of dreadfully realistic, corpse-like sex dolls, I saw a familiar flaming phoenix logo.

"Hank," I said. "Stay here with Marco and wait for Cody. I'll be right back."

"But you said we oughta stay together," Hank said, scarred brows knitting anxiously. His anxiety clearly wasn't limited to my personal safety.

"Marco," I said, more for Hank's benefit than my own. "Try to keep the girls off him while I'm gone."

"I'm not making any promises," Marco said. "You know how they are."

I smiled, trying to bury my own anxiety. I knew what was coming and wasn't happy about it. But the man behind that phoenix logo had the resources to help us get out of the country and might be persuaded to use them. He was also one of the only people in this room who I wouldn't mind putting in the crosshairs of not one but two groups of killers.

I walked down the aisle, passing girls posing with eager fans and banners advertising surefire ways to double your online traffic. I could sense a ripple of recognition as I walked, but nobody stopped me.

The tiny Latina working the booth looked appallingly young. Her narrow chest was flat as a boy's and she stood with a childish, swayback posture. The bruises on her neck were so faded that I might not have noticed if I didn't know what to look for. Below the image of the phoenix, the banner hanging above her head said *ASPHYXXX* in gory, dripping death metal lettering.

"Is Damian here?" I asked her.

"He is back in one minute," she replied, holding up one finger. She had a Brazilian accent so thick that I only really understood her from context.

I waited.

Here's the deal with Damian Damnation. He's the right wing's worst nightmare, everything they love to hate about porn in one loud, brash, Satanic package. He was just getting into the business when I got out, surfing the wave of the new extreme hardcore subgenre with raunchy, brutally violent series like *Full Throttle*, *Choke it Down* and the oh-so-sexy and creatively named *Make Her Puke!* He was a spoiled rich kid who'd never had to work a day in his life, and despite that fact he seemed hell-bent on publicly humiliating his wealthy parents on a daily basis. Always pushing the limits, flogging the freedom of speech routine till it bled, but underneath all the self-important oppressed genius bluster, the truth was that his stuff just wasn't very good. Badly shot, carelessly edited and cheaply produced. Plus he was notorious for crossing lines. He'd been arrested twice for obscenity, but it didn't stick and after his last trial he'd moved down to Sao Paulo, where the rules were less stringent. Amazingly enough I actually knew girls who wanted to work with him. I'd never been one of them.

But Damian wasn't the type to take "fuck off" for an answer. He'd been pestering me to shoot with him for years, and the more I told him no, the more determined he became. Well, now we'd find out if the offer still stood.

"Angel Dare?"

He was maybe 5'5" in his big stompy boots, one of those skinny little fuckers with a huge cock, the kind you think is gonna fall on his face from the weight of his hard-on. He wore his usual uniform of an obnoxious Satanically themed t-shirt, ill-fitting leather pants and ten pounds of gothy, skull-shaped jewelry. He had devilish red contact lenses coloring his perpetual pot-head squint and had shaved off all his thinning hair since the last time I saw him.

"Hello, Damian," I said.

"Angel Fucking Dare," he said. "Dude, I thought you were dead."

"Me, too," I told him. "Is there somewhere we can talk?"

"Step into my office," he said, motioning to the small private changing area set up for the girls.

"I don't have a lot of time, so I'll just cut to the chase," I said. "I need to get out of here. Out of the country. ASAP."

Damian was an asshole—but he did have a private plane.

"Okay," he said. "We might be able to work something out."

"I'll shoot for you," I said. "Five scenes, no holes barred, no charge. I have two friends that need to come with me too. You take us with you when you fly back home. Deal?"

"Well, I don't know," he said, suddenly cagey. "You haven't been on camera in nearly ten years. I'm gonna need to make sure you've still got it. You understand. It's just business, Angel."

I knew he was gonna say that, but it still infuriated me.

"Of course," I said. By then he was already unbuckling his pants.

Damian's favorite trick was to stuff his cock all the way down a woman's throat and then use his hand to squeeze her esophagus and jack himself off inside it. I'd done worse for less.

Over the course of my "audition," I had moments when I felt cold and efficient, like a robot diligently executing a task too dangerous for humans. But there were other moments, bad moments, when I was overwhelmed with pure, animalistic panic, oxygen-deprived brain screaming, demanding that I fight for air.

I didn't fight him. I got through it.

"Yeah, okay," he was saying as he wiped himself off on some girl's crumpled pink t-shirt. "I gotta make some calls," he said. "Give me your number and I'll call you after the show closes down and let you know if I'm able to work something out."

That "if" made me want to punch him in the face.

"I don't have a phone right now," I said. My voice felt like it had been crushed down to a rough whisper.

"Oh, well." He shrugged. "I don't know what to tell you."

"Okay, look, here's what I'll do," I said. "I'll be in the lobby of the Four Queens, standing by the registration desk, at six tonight. Call the desk, describe me to the clerk, and ask them to put me on."

He pulled out a Blackberry and swiftly thumbed this information on the tiny keyboard. "Four Queens. Six PM. Gotcha."

"Give me your number," I said. "In case anything changes. I can call from a payphone."

He handed me a business card that looked like a Slayer album cover, then turned away and left without another word.

There was a mirror leaning against the vinyl partition on the other side of the narrow enclosed space. I didn't look in it as I left.

28.

The women's bathroom was full of giggling, gossiping talent. They all got quiet when I came in. I ignored them, bending over the sink to splash water on my face. I still didn't want to look in the mirror.

One of the girls, a curvy brunette with a sleeve of tattooed orchids, sidled shyly over to me and opened her purse. She looked familiar. Raven? Roxy, maybe? For a weird moment, I though she was gonna ask for my autograph. Instead, she pulled out a small bottle of Listerine and offered it to me without comment.

As much as I hated dealing with all the bullshit in the industry, that small kindness made me miss it with a hollow, hopeless ache. I didn't just miss the business, I missed my life. I missed the person I used to be more than anyone else I'd lost. Was I really gonna be able to start over somewhere in South America? Make a new life? Find a new person to be?

I couldn't think that far ahead. All I could do was concentrate on getting Cody out of harm's way, like I'd promised. I accepted the mouthwash and took a slug, swished it then spat it out and handed the bottle back. She gave me a wink and teetered away on ten-inch plastic platform heels.

I found Hank and Cody standing by Marco's booth.

"Everything okay?" Hank asked, looking like he wanted to fold me up and put me in his pocket.

"Fine," I said, willing it to be true. "Cody?"

"Sure," he said. "I mean, it was cool, but it was kinda weird too, knowing all those people are watching. I've messed around with a video camera before, but never so other people could see it. Anyway, Cherise said I did pretty good."

"Glad to hear it," I said. "Now I have a plan to get us out of the country, but we have to go back to the Four Queens for a few hours. As long as none of our pals see us leave and follow us, we should be safe there until I get word from Damian."

We wove a zigzagging path across the show floor, working our way towards the back exit, but got stuck waiting while the aisle was blocked by a smiling fan having his photo taken with three girls in Phat Azz t-shirts and booty shorts. That's when I spotted the Croatians.

They had finally made it through the crowd of eager fans and were standing over by the Vixen booth. They were the only men in the room without big dumb smiles on their faces. They hadn't noticed us yet, but that wouldn't last if we didn't get the hell out of there, pronto.

A squeaky Asian girl with huge implants started tossing DVDs into a large cheering crowd, causing a convenient distraction between us and them. I took Hank and Cody by their respective arms and indicated the Croatians with my chin. The three of us silently reversed direction and headed for an unmarked door on the far left of the hall.

The door led to concrete fire stairs. The only way to go was up.

When we reached the next level, the steel door on the landing led to an ugly, utilitarian hallway nothing like the tacky flash and glamour of the hotel's public areas. We passed a freight elevator and a seemingly abandoned room service cart before we hit a dog leg in the corridor. I'd lost all sense of direction and had no idea where we were headed, but figured we'd have to find a way out eventually. Preferably before we ran into any kind of security personnel who would want to know what the hell we were doing in there.

We followed the twists and turns until the hallway dead-ended at another large steel door. The door led us to the main casino floor, just ten feet away from the hall where the auditions for Team Kenner were taking place. I kept Cody turned away from the AAFC signs and led him swiftly towards the exit.

We got lucky and were able to grab a cab right away. I explained about Damian on the way.

"Brazil?" Cody said. "I don't know."

Hank, on the other hand, seized on the idea immediately.

"Yeah, that's great," he said. "Getúlio Azevedo's an old friend of mine. You can sharpen your jujitsu at his dojo for a few years, get a few local wins under your belt and then after this business has died down, you can come back to the States ready to kick ass and take names."

"Man," Cody said. "It's all kind of overwhelming."

"Don't worry about the big picture right now," I said. "The first step is getting on that plane."

When we got back to the suite, Cody was like a zombie, shell-shocked and silent. He went into the bedroom he'd claimed and closed the door without comment.

Hank started after him but I took Hank's arm, shook my head.

"Let him alone," I said. "He needs time to process everything that's happened."

"Okay," Hank said. He turned in towards me and put an arm around my waist. "What about you? You gonna be all right?"

"I have no idea what that even means," I told him. "But don't worry about me."

"You know," Hank said. "You're the bravest person I've ever met."

Was I brave? Or just so numb and broken that I didn't care what happened to me anymore?

Hank sat on the sofa and pulled me down with him, folding me into his arms. My immediate instinct was to turn the embrace sexual. To take the wheel and move things back into my area of expertise. Sex for me has always been so easy. Men are simple mechanisms, comforting in their predictability. But with Hank, my bedroom black belt was meaningless.

And this other thing, this complex, slippery emotional bond forming between us, it felt like drowning. I kept on telling myself that it was his thing, not mine. That I was just being polite, trying not to hurt his feelings. I needed it to be that way to keep my armor whole, to stay safe and focused.

But my heart was speeding in my tight, airless chest. There was something profoundly comforting and asexual about his touch, that weird mother hen vibe that seemed so strange coming from someone as tough and ugly as him. I wanted to push the alien comfort away like a little kid who doesn't want medicine.

And just like that, for the first time in two long years, I was bawling my eyes out. Crying for Vic, for all my dead friends. Mostly for myself, for my lost life. Hank just held me, whispering gentle nonsense to me in that gravelly Southern voice. Telling me that he would never let anyone hurt me again.

He pushed back my damp hair and kissed my face and I couldn't stop myself from pulling his mouth down on mine. I felt a hot pulse of hunger that swiftly dissolved into melancholy. He broke the kiss and held my head against his chest. His hands were shaking.

"I'm sorry," he said softly. "I wish…"

I was going to say *it's okay*, but stopped myself.

"You know, I wasn't always like this," he said. "It's partly this thing with my brain, and all these meds sure don't help, but I know I bring it on myself too. It's like… Like I don't deserve to be with a woman, after what I done."

"What do you mean?" I asked. "Why would you think that?"

"She was such a little thing," he said, eyes fixed on nothing. "Wouldn't make flyweight with a roll of quarters in each pocket. We'd been together for about a year when it started. She'd get real mad about…the problems I'd been having. Like it was some kind of reflection on her looks or her female talents. I tried to explain that didn't have nothing to do with it, but she wouldn't listen." He paused. Frowned. " 'Course, she went ahead and got herself a piece on the side. Another fighter. A real man, she said. Threw it in my face just like that. Laughing at me."

I pulled away and sat up, eyes narrowing as he continued.

"I only hit her the once," he said. "But that was all it took. A coma, the doctor said. She didn't wake up for four months." He looked down at his hands. Clenched them, trying to steady the shaking. "I felt like some kinda monster. Still do, to tell the truth. It's like any life I might have had ended in that one stupid second. Even though I'm out now, I feel like I'm still doing time in my own head."

A cold knot formed under my sternum, making it difficult to breathe. I couldn't look at him.

"Why didn't you tell me about this sooner?" I asked.

"Reckon I was afraid you'd hate me for it." He looked at me. Looked away. "You do, don't you?"

I didn't answer. I couldn't.

"Angel," he began, reaching for me. The shaking in his hands was getting worse.

"No," I said. I pulled back and stood. "No, Hank, I'm sorry, but I need a minute here."

I had been willing to accept everything else about him: the pills, the brain damage, the jealousy, the violent outbursts. But knowing that he was the kind of man who could put his girlfriend in the hospital, well, that was something else. Something much more personal.

I flashed back to my father, reaching across the dinner table and casually hitting my mother in the face, knocking her glasses into her spaghetti. My father had broken my jaw when he found out about my videos. I felt nauseous.

"Angel, please," he said, voice breaking, showing me his calloused palms. "I know what I done was wrong but…"

"Look," I said, but trailed off. I was so torn up and twisted inside that I couldn't find words. Hank reached out to me again and I flinched away. Raw anguish flared in those pale eyes for an endless moment before he closed them and turned away from me.

He got his feet under him and stood, suddenly unsteady as a drunk. Veins pulsed in his temples, sweat beading on his hairline.

"Hank?" I said.

He didn't reply, just staggered into the bathroom and kicked the door closed. Seconds later, I heard the irregular gush and splash of vomiting.

Maybe I should have gone after him, but I couldn't. I just sat there. I had no idea how I was supposed to feel about all this. I had no idea how to feel about anything anymore.

29.

I needed something to do with my hands, so I checked and cleaned my guns again, even though they were both already clean. I was done by the time I realized I had bitten my lip hard enough to make it bleed. I felt nothing.

Putting the guns away in my bag, I spotted Cody's notebook. Curious, I pulled it out and starting leafing through. It was just what he'd said. Snatches of writing, song lyrics and such, mostly about a lone, misunderstood warrior who wants love but only knows how to fight. Angry, cliché-ridden, but still weirdly poignant poems about his mother's mental illness. Training notes about how much weight was lifted and what was eaten. An unfinished letter to Thick Vic that I couldn't bear to read. I'd gone about halfway through when that unlabeled disc fell out into my lap.

I shot a look back at the closed door of Cody's bedroom. Hank was still in the bathroom. I knew it was none of my business, but curiosity got the better of me. I popped the disc into the player under the huge TV and picked up the remote.

I wasn't shocked that it turned out to be a sex video. *I've messed around with a video camera before*, he'd said. I wasn't even particularly surprised to see that Cody's co-star was Mrs. Truly Richland, the kickboxing teacher from his MMA school. The surprises came later.

The lighting was harsh and unflattering. Cody's hair was longer, falling into his eyes. He had more acne and no tattoos. He looked disturbingly young. And for good reason—if he was only eighteen now, he must've been, what, seventeen when he shot this? Sixteen?

And even though he was legal now, something about watching that video made me feel like a pervert for having fucked him myself. He was still so young. My ex-boyfriend's son. So what if he'd started it? Was I really any better than Truly?

"Hey!" Cody's voice exploded from behind me. "That's private!"

Just as he spoke, the younger, onscreen Cody delivered his pop shot and the screen went black. I reached for the remote to shut it off.

"I'm sorry," I said. "I didn't…"

Before I could hit the stop button, the screen lit up again. It was Truly again, but with a different co-star this time, an even younger redheaded kid. The scene began with the two of them hoovering up fat lines of coke before the action started.

"What the fuck?" Cody asked, coming over to sit beside me with a bewildered expression.

"Didn't you know this other scene was on the DVD?"

Cody shook his head. "I only got it a couple hours before I came to meet my dad. I didn't have time to watch past the part with me and Truly."

We watched the screen. The new kid was having wood problems.

"How old were you when you shot this?" I asked.

"Oh I don't know," he said shrugging and looking away.

"I'm serious, Cody."

"Sixteen," he said. He looked up at me, then away again. "Well…fifteen, I guess."

"Fifteen?" I said. "Jesus. How about this kid here?"

"That's Justin," he said. "He's sixteen now, but he looks way younger in this video."

"If this was made at around the same time as yours, he'd be thirteen," I said.

"Wow," Cody said. "I had no idea she was filming other guys too."

The scene with Justin ended and another one began. Truly's new co-star was Latino. He didn't have his bleached blond hair yet but I recognized him instantly. So did Cody.

And just like that, it all made sense.

"How did you get this DVD?" I asked Cody.

"I took it from Truly's office," he said. "We got into this big stupid fight. She wanted to be my manager and I didn't think that was a good idea. It's like she wanted to own me, like I was a fighting dog or something. She was acting all clingy and psycho, and doing *way* too much blow. I wasn't even that into fucking her anymore, and I definitely didn't want her in charge of my career. And I sure didn't want her to have this DVD, because I thought she might get all vindictive after I became famous and find some way to use it against me." He paused. "It was her, wasn't it? She sent those guys to the diner."

"Kinda looks that way," I said. "I bet she's got the combinations to all the lockers at the school too, doesn't she?"

"Fuck," Cody said. "Of course she does."

So there it was. I could have told her you can't own a dick like Cody's any more than you could have owned his father's. Thing is, she clearly wanted more than just his dick. She wanted to own his fists too. And if she couldn't have them, no one could.

"That fucking bitch," he said. "This is all her fault. Everything." He shook his head. "Hank told me it was stupid to fuck her but I didn't listen." He looked up, frowned. "Hey, where is he anyway?"

I nodded towards the bathroom door and told him a slightly edited version of what had happened between me and Hank.

"You didn't know about the domestic violence conviction?" Cody said. "Fuck, it was all over the boards when it happened."

"Must have missed it," I said.

"He's real torn up about it," Cody said.

"That doesn't excuse what he did."

"Of course not," Cody said. "But he would never do it again."

"Hell," I said. "He attacked you just this morning."

"That's different," Cody said. "Guys fight sometimes. It's not the same thing at all." He shook his head, adamant. "I know him. He would never hurt you."

"Look, I'm not gonna have a debate about this right now." I turned away and wrapped my arms around myself. I hadn't spoken to anyone about the violence in my family since I'd left Chicago more than twenty years ago. I hadn't been able to tell Hank; there was no way I was going to get into it with Cody.

"I should see if he's okay," Cody said. He knocked on the bathroom door. "Hank?"

Silence for a second, then a barely audible croak: "Gimme a minute."

Cody shot me a worried look. I looked at the clock. It was just after noon. Still way too early, but I couldn't stand the waiting.

I picked up the phone and pulled Damian's card from my pocket. Dialed. A recorded female voice came on.

"Please enjoy the music while your party is reached." Awful Brazilian death metal blared in my ear.

Then, Damian: "Yeah?"

"Hey," I said. "It's Angel. We need to get out of this hotel now, so I won't be reachable by phone. Can we just meet you at the airport?"

"Yeah, um..." I could hear him smoking. "Here's the thing. I'm just not shooting any MILF titles right now. Why don't you check back with me in a few months and I might have something for you."

I had to take a second to bite down on my temper. "That's fine," I said. "But we still need that ride today."

"Either of your two friends eighteen?" he asked.

"Actually, yes, one is," I said. "But they're both guys."

"Yeah, that's not gonna work." He sucked smoke, held it, then coughed. "Call me in few months."

"No," I said, trying not to let my desperation show. "There's no deal unless..."

"Oh, hey," he cut in as if I hadn't been talking, "did your friends find you? I gave them the name of the hotel you're staying at. Four Queens, right?"

Sick, icy plunge in my belly.

"What friends?" I asked.

"That scary cougar and…"

I hung up.

"We need to get out of here," I said to Cody.

There was a knock on the door.

30.

Cody and I looked at each other, frozen for a moment.

Then, through the door, a female voice: "Cody?"

Truly.

"Cody," she said again. "Open the door. I just want to talk to you."

I looked back over my shoulder at the bathroom door. Cody reached into my unzipped go-bag and pulled out the Sig.

"Cody, don't," I said, but it was too late.

He walked to the door and pulled it open and before I could blink, he had a tattooed arm around Truly's neck, the muzzle of the Sig against her temple.

Her teenage posse stood in the doorway with their hands up at shoulder level. The blond kid looked pissed enough to spit nails.

"Tell your little boys to fuck off," Cody said. "I'm not kidding, get them out of here or I'll fucking kill you."

"Okay, okay," she said. "Tito, wait out in the hall."

"But—" the angry blond began.

"Do like she says, fucker," Cody said. "Out. Now."

Tito and his buddies backed out into the hall and Cody kicked the door closed.

"Cody," Truly said. "You're hurting me."

"I'm gonna do more than that, you fucking psycho bitch," Cody said. "All of this is your fault."

"Baby, I never meant to hurt you," she said.

"Yeah, right," he replied, harsh. "Just kill my whole fucking family."

"I never told Tito and his friends to kill anybody," Truly said. "I just wanted them to scare you and get the DVD back. Things got out of hand."

"Out of hand? Things got so out of hand that you decided to set me up and hope Lovell'd kill me for you?"

"No," Truly said. "I had nothing to do with that."

"Lie to me again," Cody said, mashing the gun against her cheek. "See what happens."

"Cody," I started, but Truly cut me off.

"Okay, so I took the coke," she said. "But I didn't think Lovell would try to kill you."

Cody laughed, a hard sharp bark.

"What," he said. "You thought he'd spank me? Give me a stern talking to?"

"I just wanted to make sure no one else saw the DVD," she wailed.

"So then you admit it was wrong," Cody said. "What you did with me and all those other guys?"

"I didn't hear you complaining at the time," she said.

"I was fifteen," he said. "I didn't know any better."

"Not like now," she said. "Now you're a real man, aren't you? So much older and wiser."

"Shut the fuck up," Cody said. His voice was cracking, eyes wild.

"Certainly old enough to get the death penalty if you kill me."

"I'll fucking do it," Cody said. "I'll do it and I'll run. They won't catch me. I'll go to Brazil and train with Getúlio Azevedo and..."

"Cody," I said again. "Cody, listen to me. Don't do this."

"What?" He turned to me. "But she's responsible. She has to pay for what she did to me, to Vic and my mom. Don't you see? This is all her fault!"

I saw. Better than Cody could ever imagine. I thought of an old friend, how he'd tried to talk me out of killing the men who destroyed my life. *Revenge isn't all it's cracked up to be*, he'd said. He was so right, but I didn't listen. I couldn't. And now, in the wake of that revenge, my life had changed forever. *I* had changed forever. But would knowing what was coming have stopped me?

Of course there was one critical difference between what I had done and what Cody was about to do. I was almost forty years old when I acted on my own impulse for revenge. Cody was only eighteen. I just couldn't let him do it.

"Let her go, Cody," I said. "She's not worth it."

"How can you say that?" Cody asked. "I thought you loved my dad."

"Of course I did," I said. "But do you think your father would want you to throw your career and your whole life away for one second of revenge? Because trust me, that's a one-way road and once you're on it, there's no way back."

"But, I..."

"If you kill her," I said. "That's who you'll be until the day you die."

I couldn't tell if I was getting through to him. Truly was sweating through her thick pancake makeup.

"The AAFC would never put a murderer under contract,"

I said. "Don't you think Vic would rather see you become a famous fighter and make him proud than have you shoot some worthless bitch and then spend the rest of your life running from the law?"

That worked. I could see in his eyes that I'd finally broken through.

"Just give her the stupid DVD," I said. "Give her the DVD and walk away. And then I want you to go back to that cattle call and get your ass on that show. It's not too late. No one in that room is half the fighter you are and you know it. If you don't even try, it's like all this was for nothing."

His face was full of a thousand conflicting emotions. He looked close to tears. Truly was silent, eyes flicking back and forth between me and the gun.

Endless seconds clicked past and the three of us stood, soundless and unmoving. Then, miraculously, Cody slowly lowered his gun hand. Not a heartbeat later, Truly drove her elbow into Cody's balls and stomped down on the instep of his foot.

The gun dropped from Cody's hand as he doubled over in pain. Truly kicked the gun out of his reach, then spun and delivered a crisp, textbook-perfect kick to his temple.

Cody staggered back, but he managed to stay on his feet, shaking his head and squinting, fists raised reflexively to his cheekbones.

Truly dove for the gun. I was closer.

If I'd taken even a split second to think, it would have ended right there. I didn't. I grabbed the gun and shot Truly in the throat at point-blank range.

She fell to her knees, clawing at her neck. Fine red mist

sprayed between her fingers and she bucked forward into a crooked and undignified ass-up position, face down on the bloody, sodden carpet.

"Fuck," Cody said. "You said not to kill her."

"I said *you* shouldn't kill her," I replied.

I kicked her onto her side. Her face was dusky blue, eyes bulging. While I watched, the struggle went out of her eyes. I wanted to feel good about killing her, but I just felt tired.

"You okay, kid?" I asked Cody, tucking the Sig back into my go-bag.

He reached up to finger a rapidly swelling purple lump on the side of his head.

"I feel kinda like I might throw up."

"I'm gonna check on Hank," I said.

Outside in the hallway, I heard a sudden series of thumps. We both froze. Cody looked from me to the door and back again.

"What the hell…?"

Voices in the hallway. Croatian. Then the distinct, raspy hairball sound of a silenced gunshot, followed swiftly by another.

"Shit," Cody said.

There was no other way out of the suite. We were on the top floor and the windows were all sealed shut, to prevent high rollers who lose their shirts from taking a dive. I was tired of running. So tired I just wanted to lie down on the bloody carpet next to Truly and wait for it to be over.

Cody shoved me into the hall closet and pulled the closet door shut behind me just as the door to the suite was kicked open.

"Where is she?"

The voice from Lindsey's office. The voice of the one guy that I had walked away from, the one I had left alive. I'd taken out every other man who'd had a hand in the destruction of my life and violation of my body, but not him. Not Vukasin.

And now here he was.

31.

I stood frozen in the closet, behind the plastic bag on a hanger that had been thoughtfully provided to fill with clothes I might want laundered. I couldn't see anything that was happening in the room, but my hearing had grown so painfully sharp I was sure I could hear Cody's terrified heartbeat.

"Okay, my friend," Vukasin said. "Let's make this easy."

I could see him so clearly in my mind. His awful, tacky shirts. Wiry little body tan as an old boot. Sharp, weasely features. I could smell his hot, minty breath. I'd slept with men I didn't remember as clearly as I remembered Vukasin.

"She left," Cody said. "Her and Hank, they went back to Yuma."

I could hear something else, a slithery dragging sound followed by a thump. This sequence of sounds repeated several times in the background of the conversation.

"Is that so?" Vukasin said. "I don't think Niko believes you. And it's very important for Niko to believe you, because if he doesn't, he will cut off your dick and then feed it to you. Do we understand each other?"

"I'm telling you..." Cody began.

"Don't tell me," Vukasin said. "Tell Niko."

"They went back to Yuma," Cody said.

"You think you know how bad it would be, to have your dick cut off," Vukasin said. "But take my word, you cannot even imagine how bad it is."

"Please," Cody said. "I'm telling the truth."

"Niko," Vukasin said. "Do you think the boy is telling the truth?"

Another voice, deeper and with a stronger accent.

"I do not."

"I'm inclined to agree," Vukasin said. "Do you want to know what I think? I think she's here in this suite. Now we could search for her and find her, but that wouldn't be as much fun as making you tell us."

"You can torture me if you want," Cody said, so painfully brave and teenage tough that it made me want to cry. "But I'm telling the truth."

The kid had no idea what was coming. I did. I couldn't stay hidden and let it happen.

"Vukasin," I said, pushing the closet open. "Let him go. He has nothing to do with this. He's just a kid."

Vukasin was just like I remembered him. His usual tacky shirt had been updated to a black and red faux-goth monstrosity of roses and tribal spikes. He was also wearing latex gloves, as was Niko, who turned out to be Navy Track Suit from the motel. They both had guns, both silenced. Niko was chewing cinnamon gum that I could smell from across the room, wafting above the less pleasant odor of hot blood and recently discharged firearms. Tito and his two friends were dead and piled against the far wall, along with two uniformed security guys and someone small and female, nearly hidden beneath the larger corpses. Someone with pink leopard toenails. Madison.

The little brother stood beside the pile, also gloved. If he had a gun, it wasn't immediately visible.

"Angel!" Cody cried, raw fear in his face. "What are you doing? I wasn't gonna tell them anything."

I never wanted him to know that wasn't true.

"I know you weren't," I told him. "But I still couldn't let them hurt you."

"This is so sweet," Vukasin said. "Isn't it?"

Niko shrugged and pointed his gun at Cody. I couldn't stop my eyes from going back to that closed bathroom door, waiting for Hank to come barreling out and get killed. He didn't, but Vukasin picked up on my glance and motioned for the little brother to check it out. My whole body tensed up, heart racing as he opened the bathroom door. Nothing happened.

Hank lay curled on his side on the tile floor. The little brother toed Hank's prone form and he groaned, a dribble of bile leaking from the corner of his mouth.

"Jesus, Hank!" Cody lunged towards the bathroom. Vukasin backed him up with the silenced muzzle of his gun.

The little brother said something in Croatian and Vukasin nodded, replied.

"Okay my friends," Vukasin said. "Here's what we are going to do. Niko, give Angel your jacket."

Niko took off his track jacket and tossed it to me.

"Put it on," Vukasin said. "And zip it up."

I did like he said, zipping the jacket to cover up the blood spatter on my white tank top from shooting Truly. My shorts and sneakers were both black and didn't show blood.

"Now I'm going to open the door," Vukasin said. "And we will get into the elevator. When we reach the lobby, you are going to walk ahead of us. Take this ticket." He handed me a valet ticket and a wad of cash. "Give it to the valet and when the car is brought around, get into the passenger seat and wait. Remember that Niko will be holding your little boyfriend very close. I will be watching you, Angel, and if you fuck me, the little boyfriend is dead. Do we understand each other?"

"Yes," I said quietly. I looked back at Hank, but the little brother was squatting over him, blocking my view.

Vukasin stuck his gun down the back of his jeans and pulled the door open, motioning for me to go ahead. If you squinted you'd almost think he was a gentleman. As we walked together towards the elevators, Niko kept a mock-friendly arm around Cody, snapping his gum. When we reached the bank of elevators, Vukasin took off his gloves and handed them to Niko who took his own off and stuck them all in his pocket. The elevator arrived and down we went, casual as any other guests.

Three floors down, the elevator stopped and a chubby young girl got on. She had a pretty, friendly face and smiled at us like no one had ever hurt her.

"Hi there," she said. "How you guys doing?"

"Very well, thank you," Vukasin replied.

"Where are you from?" she asked.

"Transylvania," Vukasin said.

"Shut up! Really?" She squinted at Vukasin like she was trying to figure if he was pulling one over on her. "You are not. Are you?"

Vukasin nodded and winked. The girl blushed. My mind was running a thousand miles an hour, trying to think of a way to signal her, to subliminally force her to call the police.

"Are there really real vampires there?" she blurted out, then giggled and turned even more pink.

"Yes," Vukasin said. "There are."

Then we arrived in the lobby and the doors slid open. Vukasin motioned for the girl to go ahead.

"Enjoy your visit in America," she said.

"Oh, we will," Vukasin said. "Thank you."

We got out of the elevator. My brain was whirling a million miles an hour. What was happening back in the hotel room? Was the little brother just gonna shoot Hank dead while he lay there, defenseless? I felt such a massive crushing hopelessness I could barely breathe. I tried to focus on the one thing I might still be able to control: making sure Vukasin didn't hurt Cody.

He pushed me through the doors. An attendant came up to me with his hand outstretched and I put Vukasin's valet ticket and money in his palm. As he ran to retrieve the car, I stood there alone, wondering what Vukasin was planning to do with me. Kill me? Bring me to his boss? I tried to push these thoughts out of my mind and concentrate on figuring out a way to make him let Cody go.

I looked back over my shoulder, hoping to see what Vukasin and Niko were doing, but the doors were mirrored glass. All I could see was the pale, frozen mask that was my own face.

A car pulled up in front of me, a black Chrysler 300. That figured. The last time I'd been in a 300 with Vukasin, I was tied up in the trunk. I almost felt like I should get into the trunk now, for old time's sake.

But I got into the passenger seat like I'd been told. Vukasin appeared a moment later with Niko and Cody behind him. He pressed another couple of bills into the grinning valet's hand and then got behind the wheel. Niko and Cody climbed into the back seat.

In the rear view mirror I saw Niko grip Cody by the back of the neck, forcing the kid's head down into his lap. For a weird moment, I though he was gonna make Cody blow him, but he just pressed the gun against the back of Cody's head and held him down so his cheek rested against Niko's thigh. I took this as a good sign. If they didn't want Cody to know where we were going, maybe they would let him go.

Where we were going turned out to be one of those soulless cookie-cutter suburban developments on the outskirts of Vegas, the ones that look like fake human habitats created by aliens for an interstellar zoo. The small house Vukasin parked in front of was one of a hundred or so, all identical and mostly empty, gutted by recession. A "For Sale" sign sprouted from virtually every lawn, including the one Vukasin had chosen.

Inside it was over-air-conditioned and fully furnished in the most generic possible way. Everything was beige and you forgot what it looked like as soon as you looked away. No family photos, no personal clutter, nothing that would give any impression that real people had ever lived here.

Vukasin placed his car keys and .38 on a small table by the door as if it were his house, like he was coming home from work and ready to relax and watch television.

We were marched silently up some steps and into a large empty bedroom. Heavy-gauge clear plastic tarp covered the walls and the beige carpet. Not a good sign.

"Okay," I said fighting to keep my voice steady. "I'm here. I did everything you asked. Now let him go."

"I'm not gonna leave you, Angel," Cody said, twisting his arm against Niko's grip, all brave chin and terrified eyes.

"Please," I said. "Let him go."

"Niko," Vukasin said. "Let him go."

Niko nodded and shot Cody in the head. Twice.

32.

Before Cody's body hit the plastic I threw myself at Vukasin in a blind rage. I felt rough hands on me, wrestling me to the floor and a gun butt slamming into my face again and again, but I couldn't stop flailing, kicking and biting. Then I felt the barrel of the gun thrust between my teeth, clawing at the back of my throat and all the fight in me drained away like blood.

"She is so eager to be with me," Vukasin said, grinning and adjusting his twisted collar. "Clean her up."

Niko dragged me into a small bathroom. Vukasin held a gun on me while Niko wiped the blood off my arms and chest with cheap beige towels. I didn't fight. I felt like I was already dead.

Once I was clean everywhere he could reach with my clothes on, Niko took them off, coldly efficient with my buttons and zippers and hooks. He wet a washcloth and scrubbed between my legs, working quickly and with no wasted motion, like I was an incriminating object that needed to be wiped clean of fingerprints.

They walked me back out at gunpoint. My eye instantly went to Cody. He lay on his back, arms flung wide like a kid making a snow angel. Like he was just pretending to be dead and any minute he was gonna pop up and laugh at the look on my face. That should have hurt, but it didn't. I felt nothing.

Niko kicked me in the stomach and I stumbled backward,

gasping and falling on my ass, plastic crackling beneath me. Vukasin tossed Niko a roll of duct tape. The sight of the tape sliced through the numbness, galvanizing me to desperate action.

I hit Niko so hard that his gum flew out of his mouth. It wasn't anywhere near hard enough. He grabbed the front of my throat, pinching my larynx between his thumb and forefinger, and I was paralyzed by a black suffocating agony. Damian's little game was nothing compared to this. By the time he'd let go and I could breathe again, my right hand was duct taped to my right ankle and he was working on the left. Behind him, Vukasin was laying out a row of awful things on the floor. Dirty power tools. Hemostats. Tinsnips. I realized that what Niko had done to my throat was probably the least painful thing that was going to happen to me in the rest of my short life.

Niko pointed to my mouth and held up the duct tape, asking a question in Croatian. Vukasin shook his head and replied, holding up pliers and clicking them in the air, then put them back down and handed a long metal pole to Niko. Niko used the pole to force my legs open, attaching a bound ankle to each end.

Once I was rigged up to their satisfaction, Vukasin said something else in Croatian and Niko nodded and left the room.

"It's just like our own private movie," Vukasin said. "I should have brought a video camera. Wait a minute…"

He fumbled in his pocket and pulled out a cell phone.

"I think I can make video on my phone," he said, squinting at the screen and pushing buttons. "But I never tried it before. Ah, here we go."

He held the phone up to me where I lay on my back with my arms and legs splayed and taped to the pole.

"My very own Angel Dare movie," Vukasin said, moving the phone closer to my face.

"Fuck you." I could barely squeeze the words out through my swollen throat.

"No no," he said. "I don't like that line. Say something better. More original."

I turned my face to the side and closed my eyes. I could hear faint splashing coming through the heavy double-glazed windows. It sounded like Niko was swimming in a backyard pool. I could picture him out there, relaxing in the sun, working on his tan. The image was infuriating.

"Well," Vukasin said, pocketing the phone. "Let's move on. We have so much ground to cover. But first, let me make one thing absolutely clear." He gestured to the tools. "This is not about the fact that you testified against my former boss. That man has already been replaced by his own superiors and the business of importing women continues uninterrupted. That has nothing to do with you and I."

I didn't respond, just started rocking furiously back and forth, twisting and yanking my wrists as hard as I could. They were stuck fast and trying to move under the duct tape was excruciating, but I was able to move away from him using my shoulder muscles like Hank had taught us in his grappling class. Vukasin watched with an amused smirk. We both knew I was wasting energy. I couldn't open the door, couldn't get away, all I could do was entertain that fucker with my pathetic squirming. I needed to concentrate on getting a hand free. Not that I had any idea what I was going to do with the hand once it was free, but it was better than thinking about those power tools.

"What do you know about penis reconstruction surgery?" Vukasin asked. I paused in my struggle and looked up at him, confused, but he didn't wait for me to answer. "I won't bore you with all the complicated details. What I will say is that it is humiliating, excruciatingly painful, and the result quite ugly. As I'm sure you recall, I was deported back to Croatia after my traumatic injury, and while I do not wish to speak badly of my beloved country, we are not known for the skill of our plastic surgeons." He put his hand on his crotch. "But rest assured that what they gave me is fully functional, with the help of a surgically implanted pump. I promise you won't even know the difference."

Jesus. When I left him at the mercy of the enslaved women he had abused for so long, I assumed they would kill him. During the trial, I heard that he had been severely injured, but I guess the exact details weren't relevant to my case. I had no idea what the girls had actually done. I had to admit there was an awful kind of poetry to it.

"I could have killed you," I said hoarsely, painfully. "I could have, but I didn't. I let you live. You can't blame me for what those girls did to you."

"Women like that are animals, like dogs," he said. "You bound me and left me to be mauled by starving dogs. For this, I do not blame the dogs. I blame you. There can be no forgiveness for what you allowed to be done to me. This is personal, Angel. You of all people should understand."

He picked up a soldering iron. It was plugged into the wall, and its tip was glowing.

I started to scream then. It felt like broken glass in my throat and was barely louder than the hiss of a beer bottle being opened. I started squirming away from him again, as quickly as my body could go. I was also twisting my knees fiercely inward, trying desperately to close my open legs. It felt like the tendons were close to tearing.

I noticed the door behind Vukasin easing open but was too busy screaming to pay much attention.

It was Hank.

33.

When I saw Hank's face, my scream got swallowed up in a sort of shocked hiccup. A hot flare of childish hope swelled inside my chest, making it hard to breathe.

Then I looked down and saw that his hands were duct-taped together.

The little brother stepped out from behind Hank and spoke to Vukasin in Croatian. Vukasin replied, gesturing with the soldering iron. The little brother kicked Hank in the lower back, causing him to tumble face first to the plastic-covered floor. The little brother grabbed the roll of duct tape, binding Hank's ankles, then swiftly made himself scarce without another word. Maybe going to join Niko in the pool.

"Here is your hero, Angel." Vukasin said, pointing with the soldering iron. "Your white knight come to save you from the evil vampire."

Hank struggled to lift his head. His face was slick with sweat, eyes unfocused. His head dropped back down like its weight was more than he could bear.

"Hank?" I cried. "Jesus, Hank!"

He didn't move.

"Some hero," Vukasin said.

Not Hank, too. I'd already gotten Cody killed; did every single person who'd ever gotten close to me have to come along for the ride?

Vukasin regarded us both, then put the soldering iron

back in its holder and started perusing the other tools at his disposal. Eventually he decided on a simple straight razor and stood over Hank's prone body.

Hank rolled on his side, shook his head and twisted his wrists against his belly, saying something too slushy to understand. Who knew how many pills he had taken, or what was really going on inside his damaged brain? Vukasin gave Hank's arm a curious slice with the razor and Hank bellowed, bucking away from the pain.

"Speak to me, hero." Vukasin asked. "Tell me I am evil and that you will do anything to save your true love."

"She don't love me," Hank slurred. "But I don't give a damn. I love her."

"Ah," Vukasin said. "So romantic. Everyone loves you, Angel. Even me, in my own special way."

He turned back to Hank and the second he did, I fixed my eye on a shiny scalpel about three feet from my right fingertips and started inching my way towards it.

"And so what now, hero?" Vukasin asked.

He slashed at Hank's face with the razor. Hank wrenched himself away, grimly silent, blood like tears on his cheek.

"Now you get to watch me fuck your woman and then take her apart," Vukasin continued.

"I ain't gonna let you touch her," Hank said, his voice hard, more focused now.

"Oh that's a good one," Vukasin said. "You won't let me."

"That's a promise," Hank said.

I worked my way closer to the scalpel. A foot away. Six inches.

"Or maybe I'll let her watch me take you apart first,"

Vukasin said. "You heard how she screamed for you just now. Clearly she cares if you live or die. Knowing that is going to make killing you that much more enjoyable."

I had the scalpel. I held onto it so tightly that my sweaty fingers ached. I started to work my way towards Vukasin.

I heard Hank hiss and grunt and could see him thrashing, but Vukasin had his back to me, his body blocking my view of whatever he was doing. I knew whatever it was, it had to hurt. Another louder but desperately stifled noise from Hank, this one longer and more drawn out. I moved closer to Vukasin. Closer.

"What do you think of your hero now, Angel?" Vukasin asked.

I drove the scalpel into the soft indentation on the side of his left ankle, just behind the Achilles tendon.

He screamed and spun towards me, blood-flecked razor held high.

Hank raised his bound feet and kicked out at the backs of Vukasin's knees, causing Vukasin to fall backwards on top of him. The razor tumbled from Vukasin's hand. Hank swept his bound arms up and over Vukasin's head, and around his neck.

They struggled and flailed together. Vukasin's flying feet knocked the soldering iron from its stand. The iron fell a few feet to my right, melting a large, smoking hole in the plastic tarp. Hank and Vukasin continued to thrash, but all I could see was that soldering iron. I inched towards it, tipping my right side down and reaching hard with my aching fingers. Almost, almost— And then I had it.

The stink of melting duct tape was awful but it was nowhere near as awful as the feel of it against my skin. I didn't care. All I cared about was getting free.

It only took a few seconds to burn through the duct tape around my right hand and foot, along with several layers of skin. I quickly freed my other hand and foot and then cast a quick glance over at where Vukasin and Hank were still grappling. Vukasin had managed to grab the straight razor again and was slashing deeply and repeatedly into the artery on the inside of Hank's thigh while screaming in Croatian at the top of his lungs. Hank held him from behind, grimly fighting to get his forearm up under Vukasin's chin and cut off his air. Blood poured like a faucet from the right cuff of Hank's pants but he didn't make a sound. He kept on working that forearm until it finally locked into place, then rolled over so that Vukasin was face-down beneath him. Hank bent his bound legs and pressed his knees down against Vukasin's spine while pulling the Croatian's head up and back. Vukasin went silent and the razor dropped from his hand as he reached up to claw at Hank's arm.

"Reckon one of us is gonna go to sleep pretty soon," Hank said. He looked up at me. His face was no longer flushed, but horribly pale. He was dying, bleeding out, but his voice was clear and calm. "Don't know if it'll be him or me, but I'd just as soon have you out of here either way."

I could hear Niko calling out, thundering up the stairs.

"I can't just leave you here," I said.

"You got no choice," he said. "If you stay we both die."

He was right, and I did it, but that didn't make it any easier, leaving him.

I made it into the bathroom just as Niko and the little brother burst in through the door.

I locked the bathroom door behind me and ran to the window. I could hear scuffles and thumps from the bedroom behind me. I tried not to think about anything but getting that window open.

It wasn't a bad jump down to the backyard. I was able to hit the flowerbed instead of the cement pool deck and the second I was down, I grabbed a wet blue towel to wrap around my naked body. The yard was surrounded by a cement-block wall. A quick look around made it clear the only way out would be back through the house.

The sliding glass door leading into the downstairs living room was open. Inside, I could hear the fighting and crashing continuing upstairs, then an abrupt silence. Niko's track suit and white t-shirt were neatly folded on the nubbly beige couch. I grabbed them, along with his narrow leather fanny pack. Vukasin's car keys were just where he'd left them but the .38 was gone.

I was pulling on the t-shirt when Niko came charging down the stairs in nothing but a tiny red Speedo bathing suit. Most guys who wear a Speedo really shouldn't, but he looked pretty good in it. He had Vukasin's .38 in his hand. I ran.

I shoved the front door open and bolted for the car. The jacket slipped out of my grasp as I ran, but I managed to keep Niko's pants scrunched up under my arm.

The leather seat in Vukasin's car was sticky and hot under my naked ass as I jammed the key in the ignition and hit the gas. In the rearview I saw Niko come through the door, then the little brother and Vukasin, answering the question of who had gone to sleep first.

I drove away without looking back again.

34.

I was sitting in a stolen car, my third that week, waiting. Several months had passed since I drove away from that little house outside Las Vegas, but it could have been one night. The same night lived over and over again. It wasn't even really living, just endless running, like a hamster on a locked exercise wheel. Always running and getting nowhere. No sign of Vukasin, but I still had to keep on running—not just to keep him from finding me, because whenever I stopped, I started to remember.

The car was parked in the lot of a mid-sized strip mall, occupied by the same familiar, forgettable franchise businesses you'd find anywhere in the country. There was only one I was interested in. A Mail Boxes Etc. tucked in between a dry cleaners and a Starbucks.

Finally, the UPS truck I'd been waiting for pulled up out front, blocking traffic and cutting off several annoyed mid-morning coffee junkies from their fix. The driver was a short black man who made up for his lack of stature with muscle-bound width. I'd been watching him for a week and recognized him, knew his routine. According to the tag on his brown UPS uniform shirt, his name was André, and he always stopped in the Starbucks for a Skinny Latte after his 10:45 delivery. I wondered if today was the day, if my package was part of the teetering stack that André was dollying into the mailbox place.

I was taking a pretty big risk to get that package. I'd ordered it online, paid for it with a stolen credit card and had it delivered here, to a box rented under a fake name. I'd scouted the place for days before that, making sure it was safe, familiarizing myself with the routines of the people who worked there and the people who came in to get their mail. Nothing remarkable, nothing out of the ordinary, but I kept watching anyway, just to be sure. Even with all my precautions, I was still exposing myself by coming back to the same place every day, and I'd still created a paper trail no matter how convoluted. Stupid, I know. But that's how bad I wanted what was in that package.

André was taking his time, flirting with the pretty, barely legal Korean girl behind the counter. Eventually, he signed over the stack of packages and headed to the Starbucks. I waited until he had his coffee, got back in his truck and drove away before I went in. I didn't take off my sunglasses.

I unlocked box number 213. Inside was a small paper slip informing me I had a package. I handed the slip to the pretty girl and she gave me a stiff cardboard envelope with an Arizona return address. I scrawled an unreadable signature on her clipboard and she went back to staring into her iPhone like I'd never existed. I left, silently thanking her for her attention deficit disorder. I never saw her again.

I carried that package around with me for weeks, unopened. I'd take it out of my go-bag every so often, turning it over and over in my hands, but I couldn't bring myself to break the seal. Not until the tail end of another endless, sleepless night in another forgettable motel.

It was still dark, but not for long. The parking lot outside my single dirty window was full of cars but devoid of activity. The couple in the next room had been engaged in howling, wall-thumping theatrics for hours, but they'd finally fallen silent about twenty minutes earlier. No signs of life anywhere in the complex. I could have been the last living human on Earth.

I took the package out, turned it over and picked at the now peeling label. I was about to put it away again, but I didn't. I tore it open.

Inside was a signed 8 x 10 print of a cowboy painting titled "After the Fight." The subject of the painting sat on a crude, splintery bench outside a rough saloon. His hat lay in the dust at his feet and there was blood on his torn shirt. He was looking down at his open hands, his face leaden with remorse and self-loathing. The subject's hair was long and dark and his clothes were from another era, but I would have recognized that face anywhere. It was Hank.

Regret. Christ, I'd been living with that particular emotion for so long it felt as intimate and familiar as my heartbeat. But was there really any kind of happily ever after that might have been, if only I'd done things differently? Or just a different shade of heartbreak?

I looked at the painting for a few more minutes, a dull ache in the hollow of my chest. When I couldn't stand to look at it anymore, I put it back in the envelope and tucked it into my bag.

I left the motel without checking out. The sun was just coming up as I pulled my latest stolen car into the early rush hour traffic. I didn't have anywhere to go. I just drove.

THE END

**Don't Let the Mystery End Here.
Try These Other Great Books From
HARD CASE CRIME!**

Hard Case Crime brings you gripping, award-winning crime fiction by best-selling authors and the hottest new writers in the field. Find out what you've been missing:

MONEY SHOT
by CHRISTA FAUST
FINALIST FOR THE EDGAR® AWARD!

They thought she'd be easy. They thought wrong.

It all began with the phone call asking former porn star Angel Dare to do one more movie. Before she knew it, she'd been shot and left for dead in the trunk of a car. But Angel is a survivor. And that means she'll get to the bottom of what's been done to her even if she has to leave a trail of bodies along the way...

PRAISE FOR THE WORK OF CHRISTA FAUST

*"Christa Faust is a fiercely original talent
[with] a stunning voice."*
— Richard Christian Matheson

*"A new young tiger...the
'First Lady' of Hard Case Crime."*
— Richard S. Prather

"An incisively and stylishly written noir thriller."
— Ramsey Campbell

**Available now at your favorite bookstore.
For more information, visit
www.HardCaseCrime.com**

**Shamus Award Winner for
Best Original Paperback Novel of the Year**

SONGS of INNOCENCE
by **RICHARD ALEAS**

Three years ago, detective John Blake solved a mystery that changed his life forever—and left a woman he loved dead. Now Blake is back, to investigate the apparent suicide of Dorothy Louise Burke, a beautiful college student with a double life. The secrets Blake uncovers could blow the lid off New York City's sex trade…if they don't kill him first.

Richard Aleas' first novel, LITTLE GIRL LOST, was among the most celebrated crime novels of the year, nominated for both the Edgar and Shamus Awards. *But nothing in John Blake's first case could prepare you for the shocking conclusion of his second…*

Raves for SONGS OF INNOCENCE:

"An instant classic."
— The Washington Post

"The best thing Hard Case is publishing right now."
— The San Francisco Chronicle

"His powerful conclusion will drop jaws."
— Publishers Weekly

"So sharp [it'll] slice your finger as you flip the pages."
— Playboy

**Available now at your favorite bookstore.
For more information, visit
www.HardCaseCrime.com**

From the Best-Selling Author of
THE FURY

BABY MOLL
by JOHN FARRIS

Six years after quitting the Florida Mob, Peter Mallory is about to be dragged back in.

Stalked by a vicious killer and losing his hold on power, Mallory's old boss needs help—the sort of help only a man like Mallory can provide. But behind the walls of the fenced-in island compound he once called home, Mallory is about to find himself surrounded by beautiful women, by temptation, and by danger—and one wrong step could trigger a bloodbath…

Acclaim for John Farris:

"A legend among thriller novelists."
— Dean Koontz

*"Farris has a genius for
creating compelling suspense."*
— Peter Benchley

*"Few writers have Mr. Farris's talent for masterfully
devious plotting, the shattering, effective use of
violence, and in-depth characterization."*
— The New York Times

"Nobody does it better."
— Stephen King

**Available now at your favorite bookstore.
For more information, visit
www.HardCaseCrime.com**

The final crime novel from
THE KING OF PULP FICTION!

DEAD STREET

by **MICKEY SPILLANE**

**PREPARED FOR PUBLICATION BY
MAX ALLAN COLLINS**

For 20 years, former NYPD cop Jack Stang has lived with the memory of his girlfriend's death in an attempted abduction. But what if she didn't actually die? What if she somehow secretly survived, but lost her sight, her memory, and everything else she had...except her enemies?

Now Jack has a second chance to save the only woman he ever loved—*or to lose her for good.*

Acclaim for Mickey Spillane:

"One of the world's most popular mystery writers."
— The Washington Post

"Spillane is a master in compelling you to always turn the next page."
— The New York Times

"A rough-hewn charm that's as refreshing as it is rare."
— Entertainment Weekly

"One of the all-time greats."
— Denver Rocky Mountain News

**Available now at your favorite bookstore.
For more information, visit
www.HardCaseCrime.com**